THE
RIDE
HOME

BY
SHARON MANIACI

The Ride Home
Written by Sharon Maniaci
Foreword by David Melton
Edited by Marla McKenna

Cover & Interior Layout by Michael Nicloy

Cover Photos by Sharon Maniaci
Author Photo by Dawn Wilcox
Book Sumary by Elizabeth Powell

ISBN: 978-1945907685

PUBLISHED BY NICO 11 PUBLISHING & DESIGN
MUKWONAGO, WISCONSIN
www.nico11publishing.com

Be well read.

Quantity orders may be made by contacting the publisher:
mike@nico11publishing.com

Printed in the United States of America

AUTHOR'S NOTE

Dearest Reader:

I want to thank you from the bottom of my heart for taking the time and diving into this story. It will not be an easy read and will have some triggering events for some of you. This is why my editor, publisher and I have all agreed to put disclaimers and warnings about the language in here.

It is, without a doubt, a very raw and very real story. The events that take place, in large part, did actually happen. The fictional portion of the story is the death of one of the characters and the events surrounding it. Some names have been changed, some have not. Those that have not been changed have been approved to remain true.

This book has been in the works since 2013. I really did begin writing as a way to heal from the trauma I experienced and the memories resurfacing after all those years. Had I not taken what turned out to be a pretty significant path in life back in 2015, I would not have met my editor, Marla McKenna. We had a brief conversation about publishing this a few years ago, I continued to write and took a break while working on my graduate degree. It wasn't until she approached me with a different project to participate in that I realized publishing this work was even possible. I even told her, had I not started a journey down one path in 2015, I would not have taken this turn and this work would have stayed tucked away in a file on my computer.

THE RIDE HOME came from a place of pain, healing and understanding. It is a labor of love in some ways, but it has become a testimony of sorts. It is part of my truth and my growth. As the story continues (yes, there is more), I hope you, the reader, will see the growth and development "Kris" has experienced.

This story is my way of finding peace and justice where I was unable to do so in the court systems. It is my way of letting anyone who has experienced sexual abuse or sexual assault know, YOU ARE NOT ALONE! It is a difficult subject to know and even more difficult to share. I always believed that "Taking the power back" was cliché, and something that was said to survivors to make them feel better. I promise, it isn't at all cliché. The first time I said it all out loud, I was no longer a victim of this trauma, I was a SURVIVOR!

If you or someone you love and care about have experienced sexual abuse or sexual assault, there are resources:

National Sexual Assault Hotline:

1-800-656-4673

National Sexual Violence Resource Center (NSVRC):

www.nsvrc.org

ACKNOWLEDGMENTS

Mom and Dad, without your encouragement, love and support in the adventures and paths I chose throughout my life, none of this would be possible. Thank you for always believing in me and helping me see that I can do anything I set my mind to. I love you both so very much and could not have asked for better parents.

To my sisters, Angie and Tricia (a.k.a. Cat and Lilly), thank you for always being there when I needed an ear, a shoulder to cry on and carry some of my weight. Thank you both for having the ability to make me laugh when all I wanted to do was cry. The quick witted comments always seem to come at just the right time. I am so deeply honored and blessed that I can call you my sisters and my friends. I love you my Seeeeesters!

David (a.k.a Tony), thank you for hanging in there with me through this entire process. I am sure it wasn't easy, especially when you weren't quite sure what was going on, but you knew when to pull back and when to hang on to me in the times I needed your strength. Even though I no longer call you 'husband', I will forever and always call you 'best friend', and I couldn't be more thrilled to do so. Thank you for writing such a beautiful forward. Your words mean more than I can ever express. I love you and I always will.

- Me

Barbara Coates, you were the other constant during this discovery and healing process and there are not enough words to begin to thank you. You too carried some of my burden when I knew you had your own to carry. True friends are hard to find, but I am thrilled that I found you through the fence. - Wilson

Kate Kolb, thank you ever so much for the love and support you have given me over the years (30 + I think...you are old as shit! HaHa). Thanks for going down to the headquarters with me and Tricia, and for the late night talks, tears, laughter and internet searches. You have an amazing soul Mary Katherine and I love you girl.

Tina Shafer (a.k.a. Adrienne), see what journaling did!!! I thank God every day for putting you in my path at just the right time. I truly needed someone like you who wouldn't let me get away with my tendencies to avoid issues. I met my match for stubbornness when I walked into your office for the first time. I have learned so much during those hours with you and am even better than I could ever have dreamed of. I also learned to be more humble and in that humility I will admit in print: the yoga worked…there, you have it in writing now. HA!

There are so many others I wish I could list individually, but it would literally take another book to do so. When I sat down late at night to start writing this book, I turned on a radio and heard the song "Dark Horse" by Katy Perry. As odd as it sounds, it fueled my fire and helped me during my healing process. (Fooled those that really know me, it wasn't a Rick Springfield song). I can relate to "Dark Horse", because I am 'capable of anything'. Selene Lambert, thank you for the many hours of Panera talks, the encouragement and spiritual support. I also want to thank the following for their role in this process: Becky (Shannon) Werner, Dina (Whelchel) Dougherty, Lawana Thompson, Karen Williamson, Eleanor Hoskins, and Dr. Lisa Leppo.

This story is dedicated to the following:

Elizabeth Powell (a.k.a. Ronnie)—I am so proud and honored to call you my friend after all these years. Your plan worked…it made me stronger and more determined than ever in many ways. Thank you for going with me to places I know you would have rather not gone. It means the world to me that you've "Got My Six", no matter what. I promise you will get to shoot someone in the next book! Love you woman.

Darren Hampton (a.k.a. Derrick) – From the bottom of my heart, thank you for being such an important part in my life, my brother in blue, and always listening to me. Thank you for helping in naming and fighting my demons, but most important of all… thank you for teaching me how to properly eat chicken wings. You will live on forever in my heart and through this story. God Speed my friend.

To all survivors of sexual abuse; sexual assault and rape. You still hold the power and it will never be taken from you.

FOREWORD

Dearest Reader,

It is with great pleasure that I introduce my very best friend, Sharon Maniaci.

I first met Sharon while on Active Duty in the Navy. My older brother set us up on somewhat of a blind date. The only thing I knew was that she was a cop from our hometown. She called me one day out of the blue, while she was on patrol. Pun intended! There was an almost immediate connection that lasts to this very day. Despite all the rocky roads that she and I have been down...some of which, you will read about, shortly...and despite our divorce, we still consider one another to be the best of friends.

Dearest Reader, I'd like to say that I hope you enjoy this story... but I can't. I wish that I could tell you it is a pleasant read...but I can't. The subject matter will probably disturb you, as it should. Having lived through the experience of Sharon remembering all of this, and seeing her reliving the trauma over, and over again, I hope that you find these events as shocking as I did, and still do. That being said, I also hope you find inspiration and strength in these pages. It has taken Sharon a long time and a tremendous amount of agonizing heartache...BUT, she found her strength to stand up, and she found her voice to cry out about her experiences. I was there when she shed the bonds that were holding her back, and I saw her rise from the depths of despair to become the woman she is today. So this story does, in fact, have a good ending.

I pray that what she went through never happens to you. But, if it does...if you are a survivor...KNOW THAT YOU AREN'T ALONE. KNOW THAT THERE IS HELP.

National Sexual Assault Hotline: 1-800-656-4673

David Melton...aka: Tony

THE RIDE HOME

CHAPTER ONE

JULY, 2012

Kris woke in a sweat, tears dried on her face. As she reached over to her left, feeling the cold empty spot, she remembered that her husband, Tony, was on deployment again. The dreams, nightmares really had started again; this time more vividly and fluid than before. Flashes of memories had been resurfacing in her mind as if they were trailers for movie playing over the last couple of years. This night was the worst. Kris had left the St. Louis Police Department 16 years ago, worked for a small town for a few months before meeting Tony, and then ended up moving to San Diego and getting married. Now, in Virginia for the last twelve years, her job with the police department felt like a lifetime ago...until the nightmares began.

JANUARY, 1994

The first week of the Academy was filled with administrative activities. Rules and Regulations of the academy and the department, getting fitted for protective vests, and the start of some of the classroom work such as Law and Special Orders. As she looked around the room at her classmates, she noticed everyone sizing each other up. There were only seven females in the class, two of which already worked for the department as dispatchers. There were a few of the men who she could already tell were less than pleased about women being a part of a "man's profession." They were former Marines and had the attitude to prove it. The one thing they all seemed to have in common, at this point, was the fact that despite outward appearances, everyone showed signs of nervousness in one form or another.

It wasn't until the second week or so when everyone had the required "uniform" and P.T. attire. That of course did not stop the class from jumping right into the physical fitness portion of the academy. On the second day of the academy, they took a beginning P.T. test, to assess their progress throughout the 16 weeks of training. This was the part Kris dreaded the most. She was not a runner despite having played softball most of her childhood and teenage years. Running a track was completely different than short sprints from base to base. It was her weakness in running that was noticed by quite a few of her classmates from the start, and some used that against her. While it bothered her, she still maintained her composure and tended to keep to herself. She formed some friendships with a couple of the men in the class and of course the women stuck together...for the most part.

When the entire class was together, the women had each other's backs, but in the locker room it was different. This is where Kris heard most of the digs about her running ability. One of women, Veronica "Ronnie" Lowell, quickly latched on and tended to prey on Kris. She seemed to pride herself on teasing and chiding Kris, often bringing her to tears, although she would have never shown it in front of anyone. At that point, Kris could have never imagined that nearly twenty years later, she would not only have reconnected with Ronnie and become friends, but that Ronnie would have been helping Kris fight for her life and her freedom from a possible prison sentence.

1976

The bathroom was poorly lit and very cramped as she changed out of her bathing suit. She was had been playing with her friend in the sprinkler that was out in the front yard. As she and her friend changed out of the wet suits, there was knock on the bathroom door and her friend's brother came in.

"Did you tell her about the game we play?" he asked her.

"No." she replied as she put her head down and started to look a little afraid. He turned to Kris as he took off his swimming shorts and began to instruct her on how to play the "game" as he and his sister often did.

2012

Kris was currently working on a second degree, this one in Anthropology, and had been seeing a therapist off and on, trying to get to the source of her anxiety, which at times had been crippling. The first person she saw, Adrienne Shiffer, worked for the military and their sessions were limited because of the way it was funded. It was a shame really because Kris was very comfortable and felt quite safe in her office. She began seeing Adrienne in 2009 on a recommendation from her and Tony's marriage counselor, whom they had been seeing as a result of Tony's infidelity.

During the sessions with Adrienne, memories of the childhood sexual abuse from a neighbor boy surfaced, as well as an attempted rape by a guy Kris attended high school with. Adrienne worked very intensely with Kris on these issues and when the sessions were put to a halt, Kris felt much more at ease and was not nearly as anxious as she had been. She did say a couple of times before the end of the sessions that she was sure Tony was cheating on her again, but she gave him the benefit of the doubt. After all, they were still seeing the marriage counselor and surely it was just the tension from the work they were doing with her.

In March of 2010, Kris received an email from the woman Tony had been unfaithful with two years prior stating she needed to speak to her. When she finally got in touch with her, the woman had informed Kris that Tony was cheating again, but this time it was with this woman's roommate. While it came as a shock to Kris in the moment, she had that gut feeling not too long before that it had been happening. Among some of the worst aspects, was the fact that Kris was told by the first woman he had cheated with, a person that at one point in time Kris considered a friend. They had let her stay with them because she was losing her home and moving to their area on a permanent basis to be with her boyfriend.

There was also the added aspect that everyone involved knew each other through an online adult website Kris and Tony had joined in an attempt to spark something that had been missing in their marriage. It was through this site that Tony met two of the three women he was unfaithful with. Kris had her suspicions about the second one but never expected it to be who it was. She was completely devastated when she received the news and was even more embarrassed because at one time she realized there were other people who knew of this before she ever did. Not a damn one of them came to her and told her. Some "friends" they turned out to be. They lived for the drama in other people's lives and capitalized on it.

Soon after this revelation, Kris went back to counseling sessions with Adrienne, however she was not allowed as many since she had previously seen her. She and Tony were also back to marriage counseling—this time with Adrienne as well. When that wrapped up, Kris was confident the cheating was done.

A while after the sessions with Adrienne ended, Kris and Tony were in a heated discussion about something and at some point, she "checked out" as Tony put it. She had not passed out, but had quickly come to a point where she would not respond to Tony, no matter what he tried. It scared him enough that he called Adrienne, which subsequently lead to a phone call to Kris (including a lengthy discussion which felt very much like an ass chewing), a trip to a doctor to make sure Kris was not having mini strokes, and to another therapist, Elaine Hutchins.

Kris had been working with Elaine for over a year and was just as comfortable with her as she had been with Adrienne. Adrienne and Elaine went to graduate school together and worked much the same way. Both were very good at keeping Kris from trying to fool herself, which she often tried just because she was happy living in that dream world and ignorant because it too was a safer place to be, even more so with these current nightmares. The fluidity and vividness of these nightmares were just as frightening as the content. Kris began living this horror all over again.

1988

She sat in the car with him in front of her house when the talking turned to kissing, and as she moved closer to him in the front seat, she felt the crook of his elbow tighten around her neck. She didn't think anything about it until she felt him grasp a handful of hair and force her head into his lap. *Oh Jesus, this isn't happening...*

May, 1994

After 16 very long weeks, Class 94-1 was preparing to graduate from the St. Louis Metropolitan Police Academy. Through tears, sweat, and sore muscles, Kris had made it through and was soon going to be a police officer for the St. Louis City Metropolitan Police Department. During the 16 weeks, the class had lost two females, both to injuries sustained during physical training. Kris was pretty upset by the one loss, not only because it happened just four days before their final P.T. test, but Brenda had been Kris' rock during the duration. She had been a U.S. Marine as well and would not let Kris give up as much as she really wanted to at times. She wasn't the only person to help Kris along the way. Kris can remember a few times when the class was made to do Indian Sprints for the duration of the P.T. and Defensive Tactics classes, more than two hours of running in line and taking turns sprinting to the front of the line and had it not been for a couple of the guys running behind her, literally carrying her as they were all sprinting, she may not have made it.

The day of the final run for the P.T. test, Kris made it across the line with just seconds to spare. She went to the locker room, stepped into the shower, put her face into her hands and cried. These were not tears of pain, frustration, or emotional hurt. They were coming from a place of pride and happiness. Against all odds and hearing doubts from others, Kris accomplished one of the most difficult tasks she had ever set out to do. She had an ex-boyfriend who had threatened to break up with her had she even applied to the academy and department. His application had never even been accepted. Her family and friends were all very proud of her, and her four-year-old nephew loved the idea that his "Aunt Kisstine" (he couldn't say his "r"s when he first started saying her name), was going to be catching bad guys.

The week prior to graduation, the entire class had received their District Assignments and names of their Field Training Officers, or FTO's for short. Kris was assigned to the Fifth District, an area that covered North Saint Louis and was often referred to as "Little Beirut" and "The Bloody Fifth." It had one of the highest homicide rates in the city, and Kris was beyond thrilled to learn that it would be where she was working. She really didn't want to work in an "easy" area, where most of the calls would consist of complaints about someone playing music too loudly by an elderly neighbor. *This is going to be good*, Kris thought to herself. It was the best way to start a career and get her feet wet.

Not only was Kris getting ready to graduate and hit the streets, but she had become friendly with one of the men who was in the class behind them. His name was Derrick Hinton, He had the most beautiful blue eyes Kris had ever seen on a man and a perfectly raspy voice that made her weak in the knees when she heard him talk. Their relationship was one of friendship at this point, but she would not have minded if it progressed into something else. Right now though, Kris was thinking of work, and after a couple of bad relationships prior to the academy, she was perfectly fine being in her apartment, alone, except for the kitten she adopted from her Aunt. The little black ball of fur, Mae, was enough for her to handle right now.

May 4, 1994

Kris put on her uniform as she did every other day over the last 16 weeks, only this time it was not the dark blue Dickie's pants and light blue Dickie's work shirt that she wore at the academy. This time it was the polyester blend, dark blue pants and the light blue, cotton shirt worn by every other patrol officer of the St. Louis Metropolitan Police Department. There was still no badge to put on it. They would get them that night at the ceremony. All the correct creases were in the shirt and pants, thanks to Derrick who was all too familiar with uniforms, as he was also in the military. Kris looked at herself in the mirror, stood up straight, and held her chin up. *You did it*, she said to herself. *This will be the start of a new life for you and it is going to be fantastic.*

May 12, 2012

Almost 20 years after the Police Academy graduation, Kris was preparing for another graduation, only this one was for her second bachelor's degree. On the advice of an instructor at the local community college and her mentor and friend, Kris began taking Anthropology courses and concentrating on taking everything that dealt with Forensic Anthropology. Since the police department, Kris felt that she found her niche, a calling to work with identifying remains and bringing closure to the deceased and their families. It was something she was always curious about, even while working in St. Louis.

Graduation this time around was bitter sweet. In March, she had come home from class and found Tony with yet another woman. This one was from the local club he worked at as a bouncer. She had instantly flown into a rage, and the yelling turned physical towards them both. By graduation, Tony had only recently moved back into the house, and the relationship was still strained. Her family was unable to make it to the graduation, as was the case with a few others since it was held over Mother's Day weekend. This sent Kris further into a funk, and despite Tony and a friend from school in attendance, she wanted nothing more than to be someplace else. The best part about the entire graduation was when she was handed her card at check-in and found out she was graduating with honors which she was not expecting at all. Despite the graduation, she still had a couple of classes she would attend during the summer months, mainly to fill in some time while Tony was deployed again and to add to her Forensic Anthropology concentration.

Kris drove up to Richmond to attend the summer classes, and she also had an appointment with Elaine. She was about an hour away from the campus and as she drove fought to stay awake.

Sleep rarely came and when it did, it did not last long thanks to the memories flooding through her mind. Class was a struggle to stay awake through as well. Copious amounts of caffeine were flowing through her veins, and when she drove the few blocks to Elaine's office she looked forward to laying her head back for a few minutes while waiting.

1995

She heard him quietly come into her bedroom and watched him take off his uniform belt, lovingly termed the "Batman Utility Belt" by all who wore it. As he turned around she closed her eyes again and felt him move closer to her. He leaned down and slowly kissed her, starting at her forehead and worked his way down to her lips. Feeling his warm breath sent chills through her body, and when he moved his mouth towards her ear, he whispered in that all too familiar raspy voice, "Morning babe. I know you are awake. I saw you watching me through the mirror."

A smile spread across both of their faces and Kris asked, "How was your evening? Uneventful I hope."

"Not really," he replied. "We had an officer involved shooting. Didn't you graduate with Ronnie Lowell?"

"Yes, is she okay?" Kris asked. Despite the academy, Kris was still concerned because the people you went to the academy with and worked alongside with were still your brothers and sisters in blue. You didn't have to like the person you worked with or for, but you always had each other's backs.

"She is extremely shaken and is sitting down in Homicide Division right now. Her partner was shot, and she shot and killed the suspect. I imagine she will be down there for a while."

Kris sat there for a minute, trying to process everything. "Derrick, when you see her tell her I hope she is okay and that I will call her soon."

"I will, I promise. I just have to figure out a way to do that since nobody knows we are seeing each other."

"I guess that does pose a slight problem." Kris and Derrick had started dating in July the previous year after running into each other at the 4th of July Fair on the Riverfront. Kris had been there with her Aunt Mary Jo, enjoying a much needed and extremely rare day off (for the fair anyway) when they stopped and talked while he was working. They had exchanged numbers and the following week, met up for drinks and dinner, but beyond that they wanted to keep their relationship private. The police department was worse than a hen house, and rumors and information spread like wildfire. There was no doubt in Kris' mind that when she went to work that afternoon, news of Ronnie's shooting would be all over the place and she was sure that some armchair quarterback would find some fault with Ronnie, as she was still a rookie and of course rookies still don't know a damn thing.

Kris sat up a little in bed and watched Derrick remove the rest of his uniform. It was 7:30 in the morning, and she realized he was there a little earlier than usual after working night shift. "Did you get relieved earlier this morning? Normally you aren't here until almost eight."

"Yeah. With the shooting, they called people in to do early relief so they could transition and get statements and not have to worry about tying up cars and keeping them out of service. I guess since you are still in bed, you are on afternoons now?"

"Yep. We transitioned yesterday, remember."

"Everything is a blur after last night. Where is Lynn?" Lynn was Kris' roommate and best friend since childhood.

Originally, Kris had an apartment by herself off Gravois, but when she learned that Lynn was moving back to the area from Indiana, they started making plans to get an apartment together. Now Kris and Lynn were living on Alaska off Grand and Bates, which was conveniently closer to Derrick's place on Compton. He frequently came to her apartment after relief on night shift. Sometimes they were quick visits just to say "hello" and "goodbye," but today, since Kris was on afternoons, she could spend some time with Derrick.

"Lynn is already at work, she had to open the store today," Kris told him. "Why do you ask?"

He leaned down, kissed her softly and deeply and said with a sly grin, "Give me five minutes to shower, and I'll show you."

In that five minutes, Kris started fading again, but felt him slide into the bed, wrap his warm arm around her kissing the back of her neck and shoulders. She felt so safe with him, as if nothing could ever happen while he was around and that if he weren't, he would still be there to catch her from falling. His hands started caressing her back and shoulders, the kissing still slow and deliberate, and she turned to face him once his hands started gently rubbing her breasts and stomach. She could not resist him any longer. He had nice, soft lips, and she loved kissing him. Even more, she thoroughly enjoyed making love to him. He was such an attentive lover, and she experienced things with him on an emotional level that she had never experienced with anyone else she had been with. Just being around him, Kris could feel the closeness they shared, but when they were physically intimate, the feeling was magnified a thousand times. They had not planned on being in an exclusive relationship, it had just worked out that way.

When Kris had originally moved into her apartment, and graduated from the academy, she had started seeing one guy who despite being divorced, still lived with his ex-wife and Kris could only take so much of that. Needless to say, that did not last long. Following that, there was a small string of lovers, usually cops, as they understood the need to blow off steam after a long evening or an evening which required an outlet for the adrenaline rush from a busy shift. Kris was also drinking more, though never on duty and never right before a shift. Her FTO was a complete asshole, as dirty as they come and was doing his best to drag Kris into being a dirty cop right along with him. It had come to the point where before each shift she would take something for headaches and something for her stomach. He was sure to tell other officers that Kris could not be trusted and was not willing to "have their backs" in sticky situations. It could not have been further from the truth, but once labeled on the department, it stuck until you "proved" yourself. It was the complete opposite from what she had expected the job to be and found comfort in the coping with booze and sex.

When she started seeing Derrick, the string of lovers stopped and Kris found herself in a much better situation. She was rooming with Lynn, had finally made it out of probationary status (only after a second FTO), and was riding on her own from time to time. She was working in the Fourth District, which covered the downtown area of St. Louis and had an amazing partner in Wanda Williams. She finally loved going into work once again and learning from Wanda. The drinking was kept to a minimum and sex was only with Derrick at this point. While they had discussed being able to see other people, neither of them did. Wanda and Lynn were the only two people who knew about their relationship, and they wanted to keep it that way.

After an hour or so, the love making stopped and Kris laid curled up against Derrick's warm body, legs still entwined, and her head on his chest listening to his heartbeat slowing down. He was rubbing her arm and back ever so lightly and shifted so he was looking at her. He lifted her chin towards him and asked curiously, "Kris, do you ever think you will get married?"

"I don't plan on it anytime soon. I have been hurt too many times and am quite comfortable where I am right now. Besides, until I find my Rhett Butler, I plan on staying single." She replied.

"Oh..." he said. A little further into the conversation, Kris said something to him and she swore she heard him respond with, "Frankly my dear, I don't give a damn." It did not even occur to Kris what he had said in that moment.

2012

Elaine opened the door to the waiting room and as they were walking back to her office she looked at Kris and said, "You look extremely tired today, what's going on?"

"The nightmares have started again, only this time they are not just flashes of information."

"Tell me about it. What's going on in these nightmares?"

Kris explained, "They are memories really, and they are vivid, like I am reliving this all over again."

"What is it that you are remembering and reliving?" Elaine asked. The tears started welling up in Kris' eyes, and her heart felt like it was going to beat out of her chest. The panic attack started, and she couldn't find the words. "Stop holding your breath, she instructed. You are going to pass out if you don't breathe. Close your eyes take a couple of deep breaths and tell me when you are ready."

A few minutes and some deep breaths later, Kris opened her eyes and said to Elaine, "I was raped by two of my co-workers."

"Can you tell me about it?"

"No" Kris replied, "not right now."

"Okay, well do me a favor then, homework really. I know you journal a lot and I want you to journal whatever it is that comes to you in these dreams. I want you to write every detail you can remember as soon as you wake up. Can you do that?"

"Yes, that I can do. I have always been pretty good at putting things to paper." (It was safer there, than out someplace where other people heard it) Towards the end of the session, Elaine reminded Kris of her being out of town the following week for a conference; however, they could schedule a phone session. A time was set for that, Kris thought how much better that would be than saying these things face to face.

1996

Kris was getting ready for work early in the morning and was running a little bit late when her phone rang. "Hey, what are you doing?" It was Derrick and she had not seen much of him lately, as the different shifts and court dates were starting to compete with their time together.

"Getting ready for work, I am on mornings and running late. It's the third time this week I will have been late and that bitch of a Sergeant I am working for is going to have my ass today." She said.

"Since you are already late, why don't you stop by my place and we can blow off some steam together." Kris looked at her watch and figured, *fuck it, what's an hour more at this point?* "Give me directions since this is the first time I have been to your place in the almost two years we have been dating," she said with a hint of venom in her voice. They were always at Kris and Lynn's apartment because Derrick's roommate was a cop who worked out of the same station house as Kris and they kept their relationship to themselves. Kris had started seeing other people on occasion, especially since she and Derrick had few moments together these days. When the job with the department wasn't keeping them apart, it was his job in the Army Reserves that was. He had been going in and out of town a lot, so Kris took advantage of their "non-exclusive" status and had started seeing another cop.

As Kris approached the house, where Derrick lived, she realized that she had in fact been there before. She had been there several times. Derrick had mentioned his roommate's name a couple of times while they were dating, and she had never connected the name until now...the other cop Kris was seeing was Derrick's roommate. Kris and Derrick made love with a fury and fervor they had not experienced in a long time. The time apart was quite noticeable this time as she climaxed almost instantly when they started and continued to do so throughout the love making.

When they finished, Kris took a quick shower, careful not to get her hair wet, since she had called into the station and told them she had a flat tire and was waiting for it to be replaced. She walked back into Derrick's bedroom and started putting on her uniform, and as she was hooking up her gun belt and putting her gun in its holster, she felt Derrick's eyes on her. She looked at him and smiled and as she did he noticed his head slightly lower, his eyes closing for a moment. She had suddenly got that feeling in the pit of her stomach, the one that told her something not good was about to happen. She stopped what she was doing, her hand still on the butt of her handgun and said, "What? What is going on that I don't know about?"

"That was nice. I really enjoyed it. It was actually very hot," he said.

He obviously wasn't going to say what he wanted, so she told him, "I am already very late for work and have to prepare for the ass chewing I am going to get from that bitch I work for. Call me later."

"Okay babe, I will talk to you soon. Oh, by the way... (*here it comes, she thought*) I got married last weekend." Kris had one hand on the doorknob and the other still on the butt of her gun.

She could feel the tears starting, her face flushing, and heart racing. She hadn't just been punched in the gut, she felt like she had been kicked in the face too, but she held it all in. "Not a smart thing to tell me when you are 10 feet away from your firearm and I have mine strapped to my hip; but you know what Derrick, that's fine. I appreciate your telling me, because oh by the way, I have been fucking your roommate too." She slammed the door shut and in doing so, woke the roommate. He opened his door, and looked at Kris and Derrick. Derrick had apparently opened his bedroom door to say something to Kris. Before Derrick could open his mouth to get the words out, Kris moved towards Derrick's roommate, kissed him hard and deep and said with a questioning tone, "See you tonight?"

He had a half-cocked grin, looked back over at Derrick and said, "Oh hell yeah." After that day, she saw Derrick only one more time.

When she made it to work that day, it was quite possibly one of the worst days of her life. She did in fact get the ass chewing she was expecting and the sergeant rode her continuously for the following weeks. A couple of her co-workers sent themselves on a mission to assist the sergeant in making Kris' life hell as well. Kris could not do a damn thing right and was back taking over the counter meds for headaches, stomach issues, and reverted to drinking during her time off. She was still seeing Derrick's roommate on occasion and when she wasn't with him, she was with some other guy, probably one she picked up in a bar. Her behavior was becoming reckless, but again, never at work. It was reckless enough that Lynn and Gina had both made mention of it to her on different occasions.

CHAPTER TWO

O ne day at work, she went to the desk to pick up her radio after roll call when she struck up a conversation with an officer by the name of Mack Parkins. He worked in the Ninth District on night shift but was on desk duty due to an injury that required minor surgery. He was good looking and easy to talk to. Over time she learned that he was the son of a Captain on the department and was apparently in an unhappy marriage. He told Kris that he worked nights because it limited the time he had to spend with his wife since she had a job during the hours he normally spent sleeping. Kris and Mack eventually started hanging out during their days off and the mornings when they were on the 3 – 11 shift. Their friendship turned into a sexual relationship quickly, and Kris really did not care that he was married. At least she knew ahead of time, and there was no chance of her getting hurt when this one ended.

In September, Kris received a call from her mom informing her that her grandmother had passed. Kris was devastated. The day she returned to work following the funeral, she was picking up her mail which included condolence cards from friends and other officers in the department. As she picked up one of the cards, she saw the word "Troll" scribbled on it. As she checked all her mail, she noticed it scribbled on every single piece of mail, including court notices that required her appearance. Silently the tears began to roll down her face just as Mack was walking up to the front desk. "I am sorry to hear about your grandma. I know you were very close with her. Maybe you should have taken another day," he said.

"It's not that. Look at this," she showed him the mail.

He put his hand on her elbow, gave a gentle squeeze and said, "Let's go have a drink after work. I will tell my wife that a co-worker needs an ear, and I will be late."

"I am not going to take you from your evening if you have things you have to do. I am pretty sure someone knows about us, and this is a result of it."

"Don't worry about it. We will go someplace out of the city and out of the way from what could be prying eyes. In the meantime, you should think about switching to permanent nights. You wouldn't be with these idiots and the best part is, your pay increases."

Later that afternoon, Kris and Mack went to a hole in the wall bar in South County and discussed her moving to the night shift. She called the station and left a message with her captain asking to have a meeting with him about transferring to nights. Within a week, she was working for a new sergeant and riding with a new partner, Andrew Smith, a very quiet, laid back former Marine Drill Instructor. He and Wanda were friends as well and Kris started to feel good about her job again, just as she did when she was with Wanda. Things were once again feeling right in Kris' life, and she loved going to work again.

July, 2012

A couple of nights passed with dreamless sleep and over the course of the weekend, the nightmares returned. It was becoming exhausting; Kris was falling behind on her readings and papers because of the lack of sleep. When will this shit ever end? Kris thought to herself. I just want this to be over, and be able to sleep without waking up screaming, sweating, and crying. She longed for Tony's comfort and his arms holding her and telling her it would all be okay. At about 2 a.m. the night before her phone session, Kris woke again and went straight to her journal. She began writing every vivid detail of the dream. As she wrote, it was as though someone else's hand was doing the writing, not believing at first what it was she was putting to paper.

I was at the bar, CODE 40 with some people from the department. It was called this because that is the code officers used with dispatchers to request a meal break. It was morning, but since I was on the night shift, mornings to them were the equivalent to being off work at 5 pm. I sat at the bar, a plate of food and a drink in front of me, shooting the breeze and talking about the night's events at work. Mack was sitting to my right and a newer officer, whose name I cannot remember at this point, was sitting on the other side of him. The conversations were about nothing, recanting the happenings of the night's events and just enjoying the company of people who shared something in common. I enjoyed winding down like this occasionally and thought about calling Lynn, my roommate, but remembered that she was working a long day at her store. I could have called Gina, but by the time she made it to the city, I would have been home and getting things done before going to bed for that night's shift. Generally, I would be awake until about 10:00 or 11:00 a.m. and set an alarm for 9:00 p.m. to get ready for my shift.

As I sat there shooting the breeze with Mack and the other guy, now nursing my second drink and allowing the ice to melt, not wanting to finish it because I had to work that night, I excused myself to the ladies' room. "Mack, would you watch my stuff so I don't have to drag it in the bathroom with me?" I asked. "Sure," he replied. The only thing I took with me was my firearm, leaving my badge case and car keys on the bar next to my plate and drink. When I returned from the ladies' room, I noticed a brand new drink sitting near my stuff, not the watered down one I had been nursing for the last 45 minutes. When I sat down, Mack said, "I ordered you a new drink, your other one was watered down."

"I know, I was doing that on purpose. I have to work tonight and don't want to drink that much. My roommate is not home today, so she cannot come get me if I have too much to drink, which leaves me to drive home." Mack pushed the drink towards me and said, "Just drink. I will give you a ride home, you can page me when you get up and we will come back and get your car. You won't be late for work, I promise." I sat there for a little bit longer and took a few sips of the drink. After a short while I looked at my watch and saw that it was already pushing into the time where I would have been winding down to get ready for bed and then reached for my keys. "Oh damn, where are my keys?" I looked around my plate and the drink and under the stool I was sitting on, thinking they may have slipped under the plate or off the bar. Mack had a shit-eating grin on his face and I said, "Give them back."

19

"Give what back?" he asked.

I said, "Give me my keys, Mack, I am tired and want to go home and go to bed." He said, "Finish your drink. I said I would give you a ride home. I am going to give _____ (the new guy) a ride too because his car is at my house. When I pick you up tonight to get your car, I will give you your keys back."

I finished my drink and we paid our tabs and I was already having a hard time focusing, thinking I should not have been feeling like this after what amounted to only two drinks and a plate of food. I have had much more to drink in the past and did not feel like this. The drink had tasted bitter and strong, which was part of the reason I did not want to finish it, but I did anyway since Mack said he would take me home and make sure I made it to work.

The three of us piled into Mack's little pick-up, with me in the middle, which was odd, since having me sit at the door to be dropped off would have made more sense. As Mack made a left onto Hampton, I asked him, "Where are you going? I thought you were taking me home."

"I have to run to the grocery store first before I forget, and my wife kills me for not getting the stuff she asked me to get." I laid my head back on the seat and closed my eyes, feeling the air come out of the vents. I was feeling so incredibly intoxicated and could barely function or focus on anything. Mack pulled in front of the grocery store and put on his emergency flashers, instructing me to stay in the truck so he did not have to find a parking space. He and _____ ran into the store, and I sat there for what seemed like forever.

They came back, laughing about something, their words all running together, not making any sense to me. He pulled back onto Hampton, again heading in the opposite direction of where he needed to be to take me home. Again, I asked, "Where are you going now? I really just want to get home."

"I said I would get you home, I just have to stop and drop _____ off at my house." As we approached the house, Mack said he wanted to go in and have a beer before we headed back to my apartment and asked _____ *if he wanted one before taking off.* "Sure." *he said.* "Mack, really, I just want to go home. I am so damn tired and can barely function at this point." *I said.*

"We will just be a few minutes, don't worry."

We went into the house and put our stuff on the couch in the front room. The room opened up and at the long end to the left of the front door was a fireplace. I placed my gun, and badge case on the mantle and asked where the bathroom was. Mack directed me to the bathroom and as I walked there, I felt like I was walking in mud, barely able to lift my feet. What the hell is wrong with me? I had never remembered feeling like this after only two drinks. I went to the bathroom, every physical act being a chore, barely able to keep my head up. When I made it out of the bathroom, I could hear the familiar sound of the magazine and chambered round being ejected from a firearm. I noticed it was my firearm and told Mack, "You already have my keys, what are you doing with my gun?"

"Making it safe," he replied.

"You don't need to make it safe, we are all cops and the only three people here. Give me my damn gun and take me to my car so I can go home!" As I walked closer to him, he put his hands on my arms and leaned in as if he was going to kiss me. "You are too drunk to drive home right now," he said as he put my hands behind me. It was then that I realized the new officer was behind me and felt the cold steel of the handcuffs hitting my wrists.

My head was swimming and I was trying to understand what was happening, and knowing what was happening at the same time. Mack started grabbing my breasts, put his hands up my shirt and undid my bra. _____ was behind me and they were both grabbing me, trying to get my shirt and bra off. One side of the handcuffs was unlocked and while _____ held onto me, Mack took my shirt off and undid his belt and pants to expose himself...

The phone chirped and Kris was startled out of her writing. It was a blocked number, meaning it was Tony, calling from either the ship or a phone in one of the ports where they were making a stop.

"Hey sailor," Kris answered.

"Well hello there. Aren't you glad it was me and not someone else on the line?" Tony asked with a giggle.

"The only other person who is supposed to call is Elaine and that isn't until later today. What time is it anyway?"

"Your time or my time? Your time it is 5 a.m. and you sound wide awake. Is everything okay?"

"Of course, it is okay, I just was not able to sleep for some reason." Things were still a little strained between the two of them since the third affair, but it was getting better. It seemed that the distance between them was doing some good, but Kris knew that at some point after his return they would be back in marriage counseling.

Knowing why she was awake, Kris did not want to divulge this to Tony because she did not want him worrying. She had already been writing in the journal for three hours now and had not finished putting the information to paper. Tony was quiet for a minute and said, "You sounded like you were startled when you answered. Are you sure you are okay?"

"I am positive babe. I am fine. I just miss you and so do the fur-babies."

"I miss all of you too Kris. I'm sorry we are deployed over our anniversary."

"No, you aren't and you will probably be someplace really cool on that day, so you won't even be thinking of it. I just wish I wasn't in class and could come meet you."

Tony said, "Me too, although we are not sure when we are pulling into the next port, which apparently is supposed to be Cannes."

Kris laughed and with a somewhat sarcastic tone replied, "Oh I know when you will be there. It will be our anniversary." They both laughed and talked a few more minutes.

"I guess I better get off here now babe. I don't want to run out of minutes on this card. I really miss you, and I will get you something really cool for our anniversary. I have already done some shopping for you and am very excited for you to see what I got."

"I really miss you too, Tony. I have to say though, the house has never been cleaner."

"I wish you would tell me what is bothering you; I hear it in your voice."

"I told you I am fine, and you don't need to worry about me right now anyway."

Tony knew there was no point in arguing with her and she could hear is concession in his sigh. "Well just make sure you have a good talk with Elaine today," Tony said.

"I will no worries."

"I love you Kris and will call when I can."

"I love you too and be safe."

After their call ended, Kris got up from the table, fixed some coffee and went to the shower. She did not have classes that day and had the afternoon to try and catch up on her journal readings and papers. Kris was taking a full load of classes for the summer semester and the classes were reading and writing intensive. At times, she marveled at how she could juggle the classes, the pets and other life events while she was alone, but more often than not, it all fell into place.

She stood in the shower, hot water running over her body, she closed her eyes, trying to keep the details of her rape out of her head for at least this little bit of time. It seemed that almost anything triggered a memory which brought out more information. All Kris longed for at this point was five minutes of peace. No thoughts or memories of that horrid day invading her, causing her to either blank out or have panic attacks. It was all so exhausting, both mentally and physically.

After a somewhat peaceful shower, Kris got dressed and spent some time with her dogs and cats, made some breakfast, and wrote out her grocery list. Being alone reminded Kris of the time when she was single, never really having anything to take care of except herself and the two cats that inhabited the apartment with her and Lynn. There were plenty of good memories of living in the city, working for the department, and spending some of the time off out at her parent's house. She missed the mixture of the hectic and quiet, especially now, when her mind raced with thoughts of the rape. The thoughts went beyond the hectic. They were terrifying, and when they started it was difficult to slow them down.

1996

Kris and Andrew were told to dress in plain clothes for this shift. The lieutenant on the night shift for Fourth District liked having at least one team in plain clothes, especially for the closing of the bars, and driving one of the unmarked cars used by the detectives. It had taken a while for Andrew and Kris to get used to each other, but once they did, they made a great team. She was still outgoing and wanted to go full force, just as she had when riding with Wanda, and he was very low keyed and let things come to them. The only time he was overtly proactive was when they were in plain clothes. They did more than answer radio calls and usually ended up with quite a bit of overtime and court appearance pay. Andrew had become like her big brother as much as he was her friend and partner. They knew each other's movements and could anticipate reactions to things they dealt with daily. She loved to tease him about his voice being a higher pitch than hers and his choice of music when he was driving. They complimented each other very well.

They were sitting at a local pizza place in the downtown area of the city having dinner with Wanda around 12:30 a.m. (the place was open 24 hours), when their radios chirped. "3425, call to assist Vice at 1227 Washington Ave. They need a female officer to respond for a search."

Andrew keyed up his mic "425, clear."

Wanda started laughing and said, "Lucky for me I just made relief and don't have to respond to that one. Good luck with that one, Maniac."

"Thanks Wanda, with friends like you, I don't need any enemies. That is your division anyway, why are you not out there playing hooker? Furthermore, why do they not have a female available for the night shift?"

"Because they are all playing 'hookers' or at other clubs trying to crack down on the crap in those." Wanda replied.

As she and Andrew paid their check and gathered up what little equipment they had, she chided Wanda. "You know if you were any kind of friend you would do this search for me. It's 'Fetish Night' and I am not looking forward to this at all."

Andrew chimed in at this point, "It's about time the rest of the 'country naiveté' left you. You are about to get a real education. Let's go." They both hugged Wanda and took off. Kris heard Wanda laughing all the way to her car.

When they arrived on scene, Kris was not disappointed by Andrew's promise for an education. She was instructed to go into the women's restroom and search the two females who had been caught engaging in sexual activity. She wasn't sure what she was to be searching since neither of them were wearing much of anything. Andrew and the vice detectives were teasing Kris because of the look on her face once the lights came on in the club. The club manager had been ordered to shut it down for the night because of the complaints about the two women and the fact that narcotics were found on someone who decided that it would be the best time to get smart with one of the vice officers.

Sgt. Handy responded as well and joined in the teasing, none of which Kris took offense to. It was all in fun and the crew that was on that night was the best she had ever worked with. As she escorted the women from the bathroom out in handcuffs, she stopped as a large table was being lowered closer to the floor and saw a woman strapped, no, chained, spread-eagle and mostly naked on the surface. At one corner of the same platform, there was a guy in a leather mask holding a whip. Laughter erupted when they saw Kris' jaw drop at what she saw, and it was just compounded when one of the women she was escorting out said to her, "I would love to see you up there so I could have my way with you. I have always wanted a female cop."

Embarrassed and mortified Kris responded with gritted teeth, "You can shut the fuck up at any point." Andrew was laughing so hard he could barely drive the few blocks to the main police station on Clark Avenue where they eventually dropped them off to the Vice Division. The following night, there was a small whip on her chair at roll call with a note that read, "Welcome to the night shift Country Mouse." It was in Wanda's handwriting, but everyone who worked the call that previous night had signed it. They were a bunch of smart asses, but Kris loved every minute of it.

2012

Sometime around 7:00 a.m., Kris curled up on the couch, turned on some music for background noise and started reading one of the many journal articles assigned for her class the next week. The breeze from outside felt good, and Kris figured that a little later she would sit out on the patio with her lunch and wait for the call from Elaine. Par for the course, Kris started falling asleep as she was reading. She gave into it this time, especially since she had already been up for the last five hours. Once again, she woke with a start after what seemed to her to only be a few minutes, but when she looked at the clock, it read 9 am. She had been asleep for a little over an hour.

All three dogs came over to her, tails wagging, as they flooded her with kisses. She sat up and put her head into her hands, letting the tears flow. After a few minutes, she wiped her eyes, got up and let the dogs outside. She grabbed her journal, a Coke, the phone, and went out to the patio. Kris and Tony's house was situated in the center of the neighborhood and they were fortunate enough to have one of the houses on a small lake. Sitting on the patio as a nice breeze blew her way was very relaxing and helped calm the anxiety that was building. As the puppies explored the yard, Kris opened her journal and picked up where she left off.

After Mack exposed himself and removed my shirt and bra, _____ put my other wrist back into the handcuff, while Mack stood there stroking himself and when I was once again secured, he put his hands on my shoulders and forced me to my knees. He grabbed the back of my head and forced his penis into my mouth. As I attempted to back away, _____ grabbed a hand full of hair and pulled with one hand, and pulled on the chain of the handcuffs with the other. Mack grabbed my face just under my chin, squeezing with just enough force and said, "You are going to suck my cock and take what I give you and then you are going to do the same for him, pointing to the new officer. It isn't like you are going anywhere, at least not until I tell you that you can."

Kris' face was hot with tears and her breath was beginning to quicken. She closed her eyes, soaking up the sun on the patio and took a deep breath. She and Elaine had been working on staying in the present, keeping Kris from blanking out, or as Adrienne and Elaine both said, disassociating. This is the act that prompted Kris to see Elaine in the first place. She had said at one point that if she was to place an official diagnosis on Kris, it would be Dissociative Disorder, Not Otherwise Specified, and elements of PTSD. She explained that when people face stressful situations their mind and body goes through a "fight or flight" response, which most people learn about in Psych. 101; however, there is a little known third response which is the "freeze" response. This is what Kris was doing when she blanked out. Sometimes it was harder and harder for Kris to get to the point where she did not just give in to the disassociation. It was quiet when it happened, and the images of the rape disappeared. It was so much easier to live in THAT moment than to deal with the memories of the horrendous act of violence committed against her. Of course, this is what she was seeing a therapist for too. Hiding behind it was not healthy and would only work for so long. It was already quite noticeable in her moods and the levels of anger she experienced were more than likely attributed to it all, and she was trying to cope in a manner that was not very useful.

A few more deep breaths and the warmth on her skin brought Kris back around. She sat staring at the lake and listened to the birds chirping and the big bullfrog making his trademarked noise, warning the other frogs of the impending doom that lurked in the form of a Grey Herron. She wiped the tears from her face, got up, walked into the house, and fixed a glass of ice water before feeding the dogs. They danced around her feet in anticipation, talking to her in yips and barks. The youngest of the three, and the smallest, threw his head back like a wolf and howled at her to hurry up. It was a funny sight watching that tiny little dog throw his head back like that. "You only think you are big and bad mister. I am going as fast as I can." Tails were wagging, and Kris swore the dogs were smiling at her.

After playing with her furry friends for a short while, Kris put them in their kennels and fixed lunch, sitting out on the patio once again. She continued to journal as she ate her lunch and waited for Elaine to call.

"Look _____, she takes the cock like any good slut does. Better I think." Mack laughed as he continued to force himself in my mouth. My wrists and shoulders were starting to hurt. I started to ask for the handcuffs to come off in the moment when Mack did not have his penis in my mouth, and when sound started to come out, he grabbed my throat, squeezing hard and making me gasp for air once again forcing himself in my mouth to the point of making me gag. As he did he said, "Didn't you learn from your parents not to talk with your mouth full? I don't remember giving you permission to talk either." I was dizzy, in pain, and the tears welled up in my eyes. I was trying not to let them flow because it was only going to fuel their fire, seeing me in this state. I could hear them both laughing, and then a deep groan from Mack as his hands pushed my head further onto him as he ejaculated in my mouth. He immediately covered my mouth and nose when he finished and said, "Swallow it all. I wouldn't want you to waste a bit of it." I had no choice since my mouth and nose were

covered. I wanted to breathe and I wanted the damn handcuffs off me. My arms were going numb, and I just wanted some sleep. I started to sit back on my knees and give my knees and legs a little relief when I felt a hand in the middle of my back, pushing me back up and I heard _____ say, "You aren't finished. Mack told you I was next."

"I'm thirsty _____, do you want another beer."

"Yeah, I'll take another." _____ replied.

"Can I have some water or soda please?" I asked.

"Not until you finish him off." Mack replied.

It started all over again. With a beer in one hand and my head in the other, _____ pushed himself in my mouth. Mack stood next to him, watching me and making sure I did as I was told. When _____ was getting ready to climax, Mack grabbed my hair at the top and tugged to let me know he had control and said, "You are going to finish him the same way you finished me. Then you can have something to drink and rest until we are ready for you."

When _____ finished, Mack brought me a glass of water and undid one of the handcuffs, but made sure he still had control of my movements. It wouldn't have been necessary because I could barely stand up. My legs were very unsteady and I was extremely dizzy. Mack walked me over to the staircase and said, "Have a seat," and when I sat down, he handcuffed my right wrist to the staircase leading up to the second floor. "Rest here, we won't be long." I leaned back on the stairs, which was only slightly more comfortable than kneeling on the floor, and closed my eyes. I just wanted sleep. I could hear Mack and _____ laughing and talking with most of the words being indistinguishable. The tears started again and inside of me someone was screaming for help.

I felt pressure on the stairs and as I opened my eyes, Mack was standing over me, still undressed and fully erect once again. "You still have too many clothes on."

"Yeah, well, I can't exactly take anything off in this condition," lifting my right hand slightly indicating the cuff.

"That's fine. I can take care of that and I have something for that smart mouth of yours too." He took off my jeans and underpants. Soon after, _____ was on the stairs as well, standing in front of me. He leaned in with his hips for me to take him in my mouth again. As I did, Mack was kneeling on one of the lower stairs and I felt his fingers inside of me. At first it was just my vagina and then I could feel him penetrating my anus as well. The tears were flowing quickly now. There was no way to stop them at this point. I heard Mack say to _____, "Let's give her mouth a rest for a while." I heard the sound of condom wrappers being opened and Mack was the first to enter me with _____ taking his turn after a minute or two. They continued taking turns on me until they climaxed and when they did, they removed the condoms and ejaculated on my face and breasts.

Mack removed the handcuff from my right wrist after he put the left one in the cuff. "Go clean up, but come right back. We are just getting started." I was barely able to walk to the bathroom but when I made it there, I ran cold water over my wrists, cleaned my face and used the toilet paper to dry off. I slowly made my way out to the living room and was led back to the stairs only this time I was cuffed with my left hand to the banister. _____ was waiting for me, stroking himself and said, "Get on your knees and suck my dick like the dirty slut you are."

"I want some sleep. I just want to go home," I said. Mack came up behind me, handed _____ another beer and condoms, grabbed my hair from the back and said, "Bitch, what did I tell you about talking? Now do what he told you."

CHAPTER THREE

2012

The phone rang again and Kris looked at the clock on her cell phone. It was 12:30, and time for her phone appointment with Elaine. She answered the phone as she dried the tears from her face. "Kris, its Elaine. Have you been crying?"

"Yes, I have. I have been writing since 2 a.m. and have only had a couple hours of sleep in between phone calls and reading articles for class."

"What's going on, tell me about it."

"I woke up again from nightmares only this time they were more fluid, so when I got out of bed I started journaling like you told me to. I have taken some breaks from it but not many. I need to get this out while it is fresh in my mind. I am hoping that by putting it to paper, it will provide me some relief and let me sleep a while."

"That is a great way to go at it and I am glad you are putting it to paper. How are you doing as you are writing? Are you able to stay in the present with it or have you blanked out at all?"

"Both, really. I started to go at one point but could feel it happening so I concentrated on everything around me. I am sitting outside and there is enough going on with the nature in my backyard that I can keep from disassociating from it."

"Good. Remember to breathe, and just be with yourself. Feel your feet on the ground, your muscles under your skin, and the pen in your hand. It will all work, I promise. Are you going to yoga any time soon?"

"There is a class tomorrow morning I will go to." Kris replied.

"That will help too. I am glad you have started doing that. Do you want to read any of the journal to me?" Elaine asked.

"It's pretty long so far, and it would probably be best if we did that in your office. I am still writing too, so I wouldn't want to keep you hanging if I only read you part of it. That is as bad as a 'to be continued...' show." Kris replied with a hint of sarcasm.

"There she is. I was wondering when the humor would poke through. It will also help you in dealing with something so difficult." Elaine said.

"Either that or I can use it to hide behind, although at this point there is no hiding." She knew Elaine was going to warn her about using the humor to cover up the pain and she wanted to let her know, that she was aware of the dangers of sinking back into all this information.

Elaine got quiet for a moment and said, "Kris, you are going to make it through this. It's okay to be angry, to hurt, cry, and I will be here to help you through all of it. You are not alone, you know that right?"

"No, actually I don't know that. I feel so fucking alone right now, and I am scared."

"Of course you are, but I am here and I was going to bring this up today anyway...I want to give you the number of a woman in my same building. She is on the other side of my office and does a type of therapy called EMDR. It stands for Eye Movement Desensitization and Reprocessing. It is used for people who have PTSD and helps in dealing with trauma in a safe, comfortable way. From what I know about it, it will help keep you from reacting to the trauma in a physical way. Her name is Shelby Rowan."

"Okay. Would I still be seeing you as well?"

"Of course. I am not going anywhere."

They talked a few more minutes and set up their next appointment for the following week. Kris waited a while, then called the number Elaine gave her for Shelby. She left a message and then went inside. She let the dogs out and pulled something out of the freezer for dinner. She found it difficult to cook for one person but was getting used to it and found a way. Kris had been eating a lot of salads and

Tilapia. Both were quick and easy to fix. As a bonus, she was losing some weight in the process. After some play time with the puppies, she went back outside while they were tuckered out on the couch and started writing again.

As I was once again performing oral sex on _____, I felt Mack inside me again, even more rough than he had been before. As he was raping me, he inserted his fingers into my anus again, laughed, and said to _____, "She's really wet now man. Take your dick out of her mouth and feel this."

_____ penetrated me with his fingers along with Mack. After they had enough of that, Mack looked at _____ and laughed saying, "You know, we might not be able to make her water tight, but we can come pretty damn close. You get the front and I will get the back." He looked at me and said, "You're going to love this. All dirty whores do." _____ laughed and said, "Let's move from the stairs. There is no point in all of us being in pain and that is going to kill my back."

"Good idea." Mack replied.

I had to practically be carried from the stairs at this point. I could not move and could feel the heaviness in my eyes. I felt as though I would pass out at any point. Mack must have seen it too because he grabbed my face and said, "Don't go anywhere. No falling asleep now. You don't want to miss any of this."

_____ sat at the edge of the couch, leaned back and I was told to climb on top of him. After he was inside of me, Mack pushed me forward into an angle that he needed me in and penetrated my anus one more time, only this time he was not using his fingers. I was not handcuffed at this point but it really didn't matter. I was not going anywhere. "Doesn't this feel good?" Mack asked. I did not respond because at this point I was numb. "I asked you a question. You have permission to answer. Doesn't this feel good?" he asked again. "No." I replied. "Wrong answer, whore. Try again. Doesn't this feel good?" "Yes." I said through the tears.

This went on for quite a while and more than once with them taking turns as to who was where, me always being between them. I heard Mack tell _____ there was only one condom left for each of them and that they were going to rest. I was on the floor and leaning against the front of the couch, my head laying back on the cushion. I tried to stand up to go to the bathroom again, but my limbs felt like weights. My mind was wondering and I felt like I was an observer in all of this. I felt something cold on my skin, thinking it was a washcloth, but when I opened my eyes, Mack was crouched down beside me, grinning from ear to ear with a nightstick in his hand. The cold I was feeling was from the brass tips on the end of the stick. The stick resembled a table leg in that it was thicker at one end in circumference than it was at the other end. The thicker end had a brass tip that was flush with the wood of the stick, while the thinner, handle end of the stick had a brass tip with a lip, almost like a baseball bat that kept the hand from slipping off.

I suddenly felt sick and wanted nothing more than to throw up. I knew what was about to happen. Mack was running the nightstick down the length of my body, stopped when he got to my pubic area, and said, "We need a break, but you are doing just fine. This won't even get soft on you." As he inserted the nightstick inside of me, my mind completely left my body.

I remember feeling as though I was hovering above it all, watching this poor woman being violated with a foreign object, a part of her uniform. I could see her tears and was screaming out to her, but she couldn't hear me. That woman was me. It wasn't until just now, as I put these details to paper, that I realized it was me who was brutally raped and humiliated by these two men. It was me who disassociated from this entire event and now, 17 years later it has surfaced and is as vivid as the day it was happening. They continued to rape me until they used the last condoms. Mack eventually took me to my car, but I don't remember actually driving home. I am pretty sure I drove home though, because my car was in front of my apartment when I woke up to get ready for work that evening. When I did wake up, I was extremely sore and still felt extremely intoxicated. I did not understand this at all because I really had not had that much to drink. My head was pounding as though I had been hit with a baseball bat, and I was unsteady on my feet. What the hell happened to me? The last thing I remember was having a drink, and some food at CODE 40, and shooting the breeze with people from the night shift.

I called into the station and told them I would not be coming in because I had a migraine and was sick to my stomach. I showered and brushed my teeth and as I dried off, wondered why my towel was already wet. I hadn't showered since the night before when I had gone into work. Maybe it just hadn't dried all the way, I thought to myself. After I finished, I crawled back into my bed. About an hour after roll call would have taken place, my pager went off and when I looked at the number, it was Mack's cell phone. I called him and he asked, "Where the hell are you?"

"Whoa, dude. First of all, you aren't my father or my supervisor and second of all, I have a damn migraine and I'm sick. I am not coming in tonight." I answered.

"You're hung over and just didn't want to come in. People saw you drinking and it doesn't look good for you to call in like that."

"I am a hell of a lot more than hung over. I still feel drunk, like I was hit by a goddamn truck and have a migraine as a result. I don't even remember driving home. Again, you are not my supervisor, and I couldn't give a shit less what people think. I would not be doing myself or Andrew any good by coming in. Furthermore, it would not be doing the city any good to have a drunk cop on the streets."

1996

"I don't want anyone driving in this shit. We are supposed to have close to two feet of snow by the end of the night. If you are a two man car, take turns napping and if you are a single cruiser, park next to another single or a two man team and stay put. If you get a call, of course answer it and if it is coded, get your asses back to your spot and stay put," Sgt. Handy instructed the squad during roll call. Kris checked the assignment sheet prior to roll call and she would be riding with Andrew tonight. While Andrew went to the restroom, Kris retrieved the radios and keys to the cruiser.

As they walked to the cruiser, Kris held the keys out to Andrew and he looked at her. "It's your turn to drive and play your white girl music." He said with a giggle in his voice.

"I'm too tired to drive tonight Andrew. Please take them."

"What is going on with you Kris? You have not been yourself for quite some time. Is there something going on you want to talk about?"

"No, I'm good." She replied.

"No offense, but you are not okay. Wanda said something to me the other day and we are really worried about you. I know you and Derrick broke up a while ago but that was his stupidity for not seeing what was there in front of him."

"Actually Andrew, I am pretty sure he proposed to me at one point and I missed it, so I am the one who screwed it up. No worries on the dating front though. I am seeing someone."

"Yes you are. I know about that too Kris. He is married and that is not going to end well. Hopefully this mood you are in lately has nothing to do with you thinking he is going to leave his wife for you."

"Andrew, I am not now nor have I ever been under the impression that Mack would leave his wife for me. It is sex, plain and simple and the last time I checked, you were not my father nor do you pay my bills, so I will ask you to stay out of it. I am a big girl, and I can handle this. Let's just get through this fucking night. You can sleep first."

The look on Andrew's face registered shock. He took the keys from her hand and walked away from her. They went to an empty parking lot and sat still for a while, car running and heat on low, and windows rolled about a quarter of the way down. Kris stared out the window as Andrew laid his head back and took a nap. She rolled her window down the rest of the way and watched the snow, actually listened to it falling and taking in the smell of the cold. Kris could feel the tears rolling out onto her cheeks getting cold. She had no clue why she was crying or why she was so damn miserable right now. She still loved working on nights, loved riding with Andrew and hanging out with him and Wanda after work, and she had great bosses.

There was some tension between her and Lynn and couldn't explain that either. She had seen Derrick once after his bombshell of an announcement. Kris and Lynn had been watching movies late into the night one evening and around 3 a.m. there was a knock at the door. It scared the hell out of both of them and as Lynn answered the door, Kris stood at the top of the stairs, gun at the ready, she mumbled "Well fuck, it's just Derrick. Hey asshole, still married and here to hurt my friend some more?" Lynn didn't wait for him to answer. She told him to shut the door and walked up the stairs. She looked at Kris and said, "I am headed to bed. If you need me I will be awake for a while."

Despite knowing Derrick was still married, he and Kris still made love that night. For Kris it was no big deal. She was still sleeping with Mack, Derrick's roommate on occasion and had been flirting with yet another married man who worked in the traffic division. They had played around a little but never actually had sex. As she stared out the window at the snow, she wondered if Andrew wasn't right in some of the things he said. Kris really did not expect any of these men to leave their wives, but maybe being involved with them was not such a good idea. She still did not think that it was the thing that was making her so miserable.

Their radio chirped and startled Kris a little, "425." Kris picked up the mic and responded, "425." "Call for a disturbance." The dispatcher gave them the address and they took off. It was a domestic disturbance, a family that was obviously tired of being cooped up. These types of calls increased when people were stuck inside because of weather. Shootings, stabbings, and physical fight calls usually increased as well. Andrew and Kris handled the call and got everyone in the house calmed down, coded it, and walked back to the car. They still had not spoken since their exchange after roll call. As they were getting into the car Kris said, "Andrew, I am sorry I snapped at you like that. You didn't do anything wrong and I had no right to jump like that."

"Kris, we really are just worried about you. Everything about you has changed, and it changed so quickly. I know you are unhappy, and I just don't know why. Neither does Wanda and we really want to help."

"Andrew, as soon as I figure it out, I will let you know. I have no clue what the fuck is wrong with me or what I am so unhappy about. I do know I am just miserable and something feels "off." I am not unhappy working with you or this crew, I am not unhappy on nights either, I am just not comfortable in that station."

"As much as I would hate to lose you as a partner, have you thought about going elsewhere?" he asked.

"I feel like whatever it is will just follow me to be honest with you Andrew. You know how shit follows you in this department. I never told you about seeing Mack, yet you knew."

He replied, "Before you say anything, NO, Wanda did not say anything to me. I heard from an officer who apparently drove past you two on a night he was working and you were off duty."

Andrew was referring to a night when Kris met Mack in a parking lot and rode around with him in his cruiser while he was working. She had taken beer to him, which she did often and would either drink with him and others from the district or just him. This particular night, it was just Kris and Mack and at one point they found a secluded (or so they thought) area near a vacant lot and while they were in the midst of their activities, Kris' foot hit the switch on the light/siren bar. It was their bad luck that another cruiser was passing the area at that exact moment. The other officer did not report them, but it still made its way to other people and apparently back to Andrew.

"Do you think it may be time to break it off with him Kris? You have been doing things you wouldn't normally do and if you get in trouble you have nobody but me, Wanda, and Sarge to have your back. He has the weight of the entire department behind him. His dad is a damn captain which means if he gets in trouble, it will mean a slap on the wrist and a brush under the rug. You will be the scape goat and may end up losing your job. I don't want to see that either."

"I have tried Andrew. I swear to God I have tried. I feel like he is always around me and always wants to know where I am. Even when I have days off, he wants to know where I am, who I am with and wants to see my face if I am anywhere in the city. If he knows I am out at my parents he still asks who I am going to be with. He has even followed me home or just showed up at my apartment if he knows Lynn is going to be gone or working during the day." Kris felt like he was an addiction to her. She was seeing other men but kept going back to him for a "fix." He was good in bed, and she enjoyed having sex with him, yet felt like something was strained in those interactions too and couldn't explain it any more than she could explain her sudden unhappiness.

They stopped at the car and looked at each other and laughed. In the time it took for them to handle the call, close to six inches of snow had piled on the windshield. "Damn Andrew, all that gabbing and coddling you did in there and now we have to clean off the windshield." He started wiping the powdery snow off the driver's side and with a massive sweep of his arm, threw the snow at Kris, covering her face with it. He laughed until he had tears coming out of his eyes and while he was still laughing, she said with a grin, "Go ahead with your funny self. I will get you at some point, you ass." The rest of the evening went well despite having returned to the same house three more times. The last time they got a call to the same place, they ended up locking people up. This meant they were in the comfort of the station for the remainder of the shift. As they made relief in the morning and walked out to their personal vehicles, Mack was leaning up against Kris' car waiting for her. "Be careful and call if you need me." Andrew said.

2012

Moments after finishing her journal writing, Kris realized exactly why she had left St. Louis Police Department. She now knew why she had suddenly become so unhappy on the job and could never explain why. She had even left for a smaller department west of St. Louis, which is where she ended up meeting Tony while he was home on leave. Kris remembered her sergeant and Andrew asking if she was okay and if she was sure she really wanted to leave St. Louis. They had noticed something was wrong, wanted to help but even then she couldn't figure out what was wrong or what she needed help with. Now, 17 years later, it all came out as she was writing. Kris ran into the house and back to her bathroom where she threw up everything she had eaten so far that day. She was shaking, crying and could not catch her breath. "Goddamn," she thought, why did I ever go off those anti-anxiety meds? Because they did more harm than good and you know it. She answered herself. She sat against the wall on the bathroom floor and sobbed for at least 45 minutes.

When she finished, she went out to the kitchen sink with a towel and put her head under the faucet and ran cold water over her neck. It was the deepest sink in the house and she didn't want to take another shower. She dried her hair and brushed her teeth then went to the grocery store. This time she picked up a steak and baked potato to go with her salad. She hated firing up the grill for herself, but figured she would throw some chicken on there too and add that to a salad the next day for lunch or dinner.

Later that afternoon Shelby called Kris back, and they set up their first appointment. She would see her on the same day she was seeing Elaine only the hour before. Kris started the grill and actually ate everything she fixed. She hadn't had much of an appetite as well as not being able to sleep. Maybe finishing her food was a sign of some sleep coming too. She finished her readings and papers for class without falling asleep and found a movie on cable to watch. She fell asleep with the T.V. on and whatever was happening in the movie bled into the beginnings of her nightmares. She suddenly jolted awake and was disoriented when she did. Once she figured out she was still at home, she got up from the couch, let the dogs out to go potty, put them back in their kennels, and crawled into bed. The sheets were nice and cool and for the first time in a long time; she was able to go back to sleep. This time she woke up to the sound of the dogs barking to get up. She rolled over and looked at the clock. It read 8:15 a.m. Finally...a little relief.

1997

It was bitterly cold outside and as par for the course, Kris and Andrew seemed to be the ones fielding all the calls while everyone else was able to stay warm in their cruisers. "K.C., did anyone ever tell you that you are bad luck sometimes?" Andrew said laughing. "I swear I have never had so many damn calls until you and I started riding together last fall. What is it about you that gets people all riled up?"

"You're lucky I guess Andrew. I wouldn't want you to sit in this car for eight hours a night and be bored, wasting away to nothing. I mean think about it Andrew, who else would they have put you with that could get you talking as much as you do now? Besides you are going to miss me when I am gone." Kris had submitted an application to a small police department west of St. Louis for the town she was raised in. She had interviewed with them a week prior and was offered a position a few days later. It was a pay cut and she would be moving back in with her parents for a while, but she was still quite unhappy and uncomfortable and figured it was because she did not want to live in the city as was a requirement for all city employees at the time.

"I will miss you Kris. You have been a good partner and I just want you to be happy. I really hope this is all works out for you."

"No worries Andrew, you can't get rid of me too easily. I will still come down here to aggravate you from time to time."

As they were driving back to the parking lot they had been sitting in, their radio chirped once again only this time it was their TAC line, meaning it was something that could bypass the dispatcher and come to them directly. Andrew picked up the mic and responded, "425."

"425, this is 412 (their sergeant on duty), could you and 425B meet me in the lot at 2211 Market?"

"425 clear. "Andrew turned to Kris and said, "Are you ready for this?"

"As ready as I will ever be."

"You do know he is going to try to talk you out of leaving right?"

"Yeah, I know what is coming, but it's time for me to go. Things are better here, but I still can't get rid of this feeling of being so uncomfortable." Sgt. Handy had retired at the end of the previous year, and now they worked for Sgt. Sewell. He too was an amazing person to work for and really cared about the people that worked for him.

As they pulled up, Andrew maneuvered the car into a position so Kris was alongside the sergeant's driver side door. Kris rolled her window down and as soon as it was down far enough Sgt. Sewell said, "So, I got a call from Wentzville asking me if I thought you would work out there. I told them they couldn't have you. Kris, are you sure this is what you want to do? Is there anything I can do to get you to stay? We can get you to another shift or district."

"Sarge, I need to go. I know that I am not unhappy on this shift with you, Andrew or anyone else in our squad, but I just can't seem to be happy here in the city anymore. I cannot explain it, but I think the move back out to that area is going to be the best for me."

"Okay, I will call them back in the morning and let them know they are going to be stealing one of my good ones. It's still not too late to change your mind. You are here until February right?"

"Yes, you get to put with me for about a month more. Andrew is going to need the rest, so it will be good for both of us." She said as she laughed while fighting back tears.

Their meeting ended with a call for an accident on the interchange between I-64 and I-70. The curve was horribly sharp and with the added ice, it was a recipe for disaster. It was close to the Mississippi River and the wind coming off the river was so bad and making it so cold that Kris and Andrew took turns directing traffic so they could thaw out every so often. As they were switching positions, a car coming through the scene of the accident misjudged the curve, was going too fast and lost control just as Andrew got close enough to pull Kris from the path of the sliding car. Kris saw it coming, but was frozen in place and couldn't will her feet to move. Andrew grabbed her the back of her coat by the collar and yanked her to the back of the patrol car. "Mother fucker!!!" she yelled as she was almost struck by the out of control car. She looked at Andrew, shaking and all she could mutter was "thanks."

"Do you need to change your pants country mouse?" he said laughing.

She playfully slapped him on the shoulder and said, "Nope. I am going to make you ride around in the car with me all night long wondering."

"You were right, I need some rest from you."

Another patrol car was able to stop the vehicle and hold it until Kris could write numerous tickets and send the driver on his way. After they finished at the scene, they settled down for a while and were actually able to rest for a few hours. They listened to radio traffic from surrounding districts for a while and heard a pretty good car chase going on in a neighboring district. They heard the officer calling a foot chase after she and her partner were in a tussle with a suspect. It wasn't until the female officer keyed up her radio and called for a supervisor and Homicide Division for an officer involved shooting that Kris recognized the voice of her academy mate, Ronnie Lowell.

CHAPTER FOUR

2013

Eight months had passed since the journal entry and in that time, Kris had been doing intense therapy with Elaine and Shelby. Tony came home from deployment the previous December and retired from the military getting a job teaching for them instead. There was still a lot of tension and the inability for Kris to fully trust Tony because of the affairs. If he was late leaving work, she wondered. If his phone rang or a text message came in, she instantly thought the worst. For the most part, things seemed to be going well though and despite therapy going well too, there were still nightmares from time to time. They were not as intense as they had been though. A week or so after Tony returned she had a really bad one and when he tried to wake her up, she swung at him. It was at this point that she had to explain what was going on. In reality she thought she would be able to hide it from him, but she did not have that kind of luck. He held her that night, and they cried together. Kris cried until she fell asleep with Tony's arms wrapped around her.

It was a Saturday and, as was par for the course, Kris woke early and fed all the four-legged babies, made some coffee, and went to the computer to play some games. For some reason she went onto the website of the police department just to see if there were still some familiar faces and to see if she could find her old partners, Wanda and Andrew. She had not spoken to Wanda in years and missed her no-nonsense personality. She was going to try and find them to see if she could reconnect with them the next time she went home. As she was perusing the site, she went to the Internal Affairs site and noticed they had a list of all the different type of reports that had been filed against officers. Oddly enough, as she scrolled down the list, there was not one claim against officers for sexual misconduct and the reports dated back at least six years.

Kris opened up a new screen on the computer and started drafting a letter…"To Col. Dixon, Internal Affairs Division and the Board of Police Commissioners, My name is Kristine Parker, but in 1994 I graduated from the police academy as Kristine Margaret Clarke." The letter continued, and she described in detail the events that took place in 1996 with Mack and the other officer in as much detail as she could remember. When it was finished, she hit the save button and put the flash drive in her book bag she took to campus. At this point Kris was working for one of the Anthropology professors at VCU as an Instructional Assistant. When she went to campus the following Tuesday for work, she went to the library and printed three copies. One for each of her therapists and one for herself. She was going to wait and think about sending it to the police department until after she read it to Elaine and Shelby. She had an appointment that afternoon with Elaine and figured she would give her a copy then.

While she and Elaine worked on the memory recovery and how she was handling that as she worked with Shelby, Elaine had still not heard the actual details of the rape. Kris was still pretty embarrassed and felt incredibly guilty about the events that took place. Here she was, entrusted to protect the citizens of St. Louis, and she could not even protect herself.

July, 1997

Kris was back "home" in Wentzville and had been working for their police department since February of that year. She often thought about trying to go back down to the city and working there again. Things were no better here, in fact she was pretty sure they were worse. She was the first female hired to the department, ever, and it was painfully obvious. It was still a very small department and had the same "small town attitude" that was present when she was growing up there. When the 4th of July rolled around, Kris was thrilled because she finally had the 4th off for the first time in three years. As she was leaving work one afternoon, one of the sergeants asked her if she would be willing to work the parade in the morning/early afternoon for overtime pay. She agreed, as she did not have plans until later in the evening anyway. She was directing traffic at one of the intersections, and as she stepped off the curb her right ankle rolled under and backwards and she heard a "pop." She managed to crawl back to the curb and called for the sergeant on her radio. He informed her she would need to drive herself to the hospital—that everyone was busy working the parade and couldn't leave.

Kris drove to the ER using her left foot (which was not an easy task and it took forever), and when she arrived she hopped on one foot towards the door. When one of the ER nurses saw her she came out with a wheelchair. "What happened and how did you get here?" the nurse asked.

"I rolled my ankle pretty bad stepping off of a curb, and I got here by driving. Apparently everyone else was too busy to come get me. I wasn't even scheduled to work, which pisses me off even more," Kris replied.

The staff at the hospital was very helpful and after X-rays were taken, the doctor came in and asked Kris, "Is there someone who can come get you? You have torn the Calcaneofibular ligament, the anterior tibiofibular ligament, and the fibularis brevis away from the fibula and the lateral malleolus of the fibula. In a nutshell, you tore a lot of major ligaments and muscle attachments away from your ankle and fibula, and you are not driving back out of here." The Dr. gave her instructions, called the sergeant himself and explained that not only should she not have driven herself to the hospital, but that there was no way he was releasing Kris until someone came to get her, and the police car parked in his ambulance bay. He also told him that someone would need to drive Kris' car home from the station as well because she was not allowed to drive for quite some time.

Kris called her parents and let them know what happened on her way home. She knew that calling them from the ER would have freaked them out and they would have rushed over to her. She was ordered to stay out of work for the next week and a half, and after that she was to be put on light duty. Kris started doing physical therapy fairly soon after the injury and was put in a walking boot. She was then put back out on the street by the end of the month. One day after work, she walked up to the mailbox and one of the neighbors, Nate Parker, was outside mowing his grass and when she waved, he shut off the mower and came over to talk to her. "Hey Kris, how is the ankle doing?"

"Still having some pain, but apparently it is good enough for me to be driving a police car around. Doesn't that make you feel safe knowing that I cannot chase you on foot if you run from me?" she said as they both laughed. While they talked more, the topic of conversation turned to dating and how difficult it was for a female cop to date because some men were either too intimidated by the position or assumed the female was a lesbian.

"You know, I have a brother about your age who lives in Washington State. He is single and I bet you two would hit it off. He is in the Navy and stationed there, but I know his time there is coming to an end by the beginning of next year. Would you like his number? I can give him yours but he is fairly shy when it comes to calling women."

"Sure, I can give him a call and see how things play out."

"Be right back, I am going to go write it down for you." Nate returned with a piece of paper and handed it to Kris that read "Tony Melton" with his number.

The following day at work, Kris was sitting on the entrance ramp to I-70 waiting for a car that was "wanted" for several felonies that had been spotted travelling towards Wentzville. As she was sitting there waiting, she picked up her cell phone and dialed Tony's number. "Hello." A male voice answered.

"Hi, Tony?"

"Yes."

"My name is Kris, and your bother Nate gave me your number and said I should call you."

"Hey Kris, he told me you might be calling soon. I'm glad you did." They talked for a while telling each other about themselves when he heard the police radio squawk behind her. "Are you at work right now?" he asked.

"Yes. I am sitting at the end of the entrance ramp to Interstate 70 waiting for a wanted vehicle. Apparently, the driver stole the car from his parents, and there are some assault charges pending too."

"Do you need me to let you go?"

"No, I can keep an eye out for it and talk for a few."

A few minutes later, out of her side mirror she saw the vehicle that was being sought. She put the car into drive and said to Tony, "Hang on a second I need to put my phone down." She called into the dispatcher and informed them she was behind the vehicle as she pulled onto the highway and put her lights on.

"Okay, I am back," she told Tony.

"I heard you tell them you were behind the car, do you need to let you go now?"

"Not just yet. I am still at the speed limit. I just need to keep letting them know my location." About thirty seconds after saying that, she had to turn on her sirens, called into the dispatcher again to let her know which mile marker she had passed and picked up her phone again. "Hey Tony, can I call you back when I get off work? I just hit 110 mph, and this is going to get ugly soon."

"Uh, yeah. Of course," he replied.

"Talk to you again soon," Kris said.

2013

Today was an easy day at work and between class and her appointment with Elaine, Kris went to the food cart located on campus and got a chicken wrap and something to drink. She had frequented the cart since her second semester at VCU. Hundreds of customers passed through there and the couple who owned the cart knew what the regulars ate and drank by face. If they had something special to offer, they would let the customer know in case they wanted to try something new. Otherwise, all the customers had to do is say they wanted their "regular." It was fresh, and it always hit the spot.

Kris sat there for quite some time chatting with the owners and some of the regular customers she had become friends with over the last couple of years. Approximately 30 minutes before her appointment time, Kris walked to her car and drove the six blocks or so to Elaine's office. She sat in the waiting room, letter in hand, and fully prepared to read it to her. Therapists really liked the idea of having a client read things aloud because it left no choice to the client in owning up to reality. If you say it out loud, it makes it true and real. Elaine opened the door to the waiting room to let Kris know she was ready for her and unlike she had done so many times before, she did not wait for Kris to get up and walk with her to the office. Kris instantly knew something was not right with Elaine. Well shit, Kris said to herself, this isn't going to be a good day.

She sat down in her normal spot on the couch, grabbed one of the pillows that she kept threatening to steal and as she was getting comfortable Elaine said, "We need to get some administrative stuff out of the way before we start."

"Okay," Kris responded with hesitancy in her voice.

"I wanted to let you know that effective immediately I am leaving my practice. It may just be for a short time, I don't know right now. I have to revisit my situation in a month or so and figure it out."

Kris looked at her with shock, but still had the presence of mind to ask, "Is your mom okay? I know you said she has had some health problems."

"She is fine, thank you for asking. Let's talk about what you are feeling right now." It was at this point when Kris couldn't speak. She instantly started crying and could not stop for forty-five minutes. She could not express the feelings of sudden abandonment and betrayal she felt. Everything she experienced in the distant and not so distant past started flashing through her mind. Scenes of being alone in her bedroom as a child wondering about what happened in the bathroom at the neighbor's house; again as a high school senior after finally getting out of the grasp of the guy who was sexually assaulting her; her college boyfriend cheating on her and leaving her; Derrick leaving her, and Tony cheating.

She had already been thrown to the wolves when she was seeing Adrienne dealing with all of those issues and now it seemed that she was going to get to deal with the details of this rape alone too. Elaine was abandoning her just like everyone else had. The words rolling through her head were not the same ones she would express to Elaine. The moment it sunk in, Kris looked at Elaine and thought, you fucking bitch. I have all of this shit I am dealing with and you are leaving me in the lurch. What really came out of Kris' mouth was the expression of disbelief and some concern for Elaine. "I get that you have to do what is best for you right now, but I don't understand at the same time. All of this shit I am working through, and I cannot do it alone."

"You are not alone Kris. Shelby is still here, and I can refer you to someone in this building if you want."

"No. I am really fucking tired of having to 'start over' in therapy. Since you really want to know what I am feeling, I am feeling like this is some bullshit and I am actually kind of pissed too. I just cannot do this alone and just like everyone else, you are leaving me too."

"It really is just going to be for a while. I don't anticipate it being a permanent thing, but I have to leave that possibility on the table. I can contact you in a month or so and see where things stand and we can go from there if you want."

With more venom than humor in her tone, Kris responded, "That's fine. It isn't like I have a choice in the matter, is it?"

1997

Kris' phone rang and when she looked at the number, her heart skipped a beat. She and Tony had talked almost every day since July. The only time they didn't talk was when he had to spend the night on his ship for his duty section. "Hey you," he said, "how is your day going so far?"

"Not bad." She replied. "I have the day off so I am just relaxing. I don't have a thing planned for the day, how about you?"

"I have to go into work later this evening. I am still on the night duty section. I wanted to let you know that I am taking leave and going to be staying with my brother Nate."

"Wow, you mean I get to meet you face to face?" she asked.

"If you really want to," he laughed.

"I actually am looking forward to it." Kris responded.

"Me too, it will be nice to put a face to the voice."

"I sent you a picture, so you have more than me at this point."

"True, but I don't think that picture does you justice. Just a feeling I have. I am going to jump off here and get some sleep. I will talk to you soon, and see you in a couple of weeks."

"Have a good night Tony, and I will talk to you soon."

A couple of weeks later, Tony came into town and walked over to meet Kris for the first time. They spent as much time as they could together, being apart only when they had to sleep at night or when Kris had to work. One day he came up to the station and took her out to lunch, bringing her flowers as well. It was the first time Kris felt this comfortable with someone since Derrick. They would stay up talking until the early hours of the morning, and she had no problem sharing every aspect of her life with him. She knew the moment she met him that he would be the man she married. The first time they made love, she felt like this was the piece of her that had been missing. She felt whole again, absolutely complete and content with whom she was. Kris was still unhappy at her current job, but there was nothing that could be done about that at the moment. There was also nothing that could be done about the fact that Kris' parents were not happy with their relationship, because during the course of the visit, it came to light that Tony was not yet divorced from his wife, but only legally separated. It created some tension from the very beginning, but Kris still knew this man would one day become her husband.

In October after Tony had returned to Washington, Kris was walking down the stairs of her parent's deck to leave for work, when she rolled her ankle…the same one she rolled on July of that same year. As she cried out in pain, sitting on the deck in the rain, her dad came out the door, and carried her back into the house. Her ankle immediately swelled up, bruised and after a trip to the hospital, she learned she not only re-injured the same ligaments and muscles as she had before, but this time she chipped a piece of bone away from the outside portion of her fibula. She was instructed by the doctors to stay out of work for a couple of weeks and then to work light duty again.

After returning from the hospital, Kris was on the phone with Tony telling him what happened when he said, "I am going to buy you a plane ticket to come up here to Seattle. Do you think your mom and dad would be okay with that?"

"Probably not, but there isn't much they can do about it. I am 27 years old, and I pay them rent. If I need to get to the airport, I will find another way, crutches and all." By the end of October, she was on a plane to Seattle, and on November 2, 1997 while on a weekend trip to Ocean Shores, Washington, Tony proposed to Kris. While Kris was thrilled and could not wait to become his wife, her parents went ballistic when she returned home and made the engagement known to everyone.

When she returned to work, they informed her she was not going to be going on light duty, but that she would be riding with yet another training officer who was hired after her. Then after an incident involving the officer and Kris' safety, she went into work and informed them that she would not ride with him any longer. When they told her she had to, that he was training her, she told them she did not need training for a third time. She especially did not need it by someone who was hired after her. The officer did not have the time in with the job that she did, considering she already had close to four years of experience. Kris began refusing to ride with him, and the Chief would send her home after he came into work. On the fifth day of this 'game', Kris went into work in her street clothes, uniform; badge and gun in hand, and laid them all down on the sergeant's desk. "I am not only NOT going to ride with him because he is unsafe, but I am not going to be working here any longer. I will not have my safety compromised for some 'cowboy cop.' Per doctor's orders: I am not even supposed to be on the street, yet this department wouldn't honor that. He flat out lied about the incident in which I got a face full of pepper spray from him, violated the rights of the person we had in handcuffs and seeing as how I didn't compromise my ethics when I worked for the City of St. Louis, I'm sure as hell not going to compromise them here!" Kris said sternly as she turned and walked out.

2013

Kris was still reeling from Elaine's announcement and while she continued to see Shelby, it was just not the same. She was used to doing the EMDR therapy with Shelby, not regular "talk" therapy. She started looking for support other places as well as the continued therapy with Shelby. Earlier in the year Kris had gone home to St. Louis for a scrapbooking weekend with her mom and sisters, and when her older sister, Catherine (Cat to her sisters and friends), started grilling her about why she hadn't been sleeping, why she seemed so upset, Kris finally told her what was going on. "Oh baby sister, I am so sorry. I don't know what to say. Who was it? Who hurt one of my sisters?"

"I cannot tell you the names. Well let me rephrase that, I WON'T tell you the names. Actually, I don't know the second name," Kris replied.

"I will get it out of you somehow, and then I will have to hunt them down and kill them for hurting my baby sister," she said with a sarcastic laugh. "Hey, Kris, at least we know why you are so fucked up now," said her big sister as she hugged her and laughed.

Now, Kris picked up the phone and dialed her big sister to lean on once again. She knew her baby sister, Lilly was working and did not want to bother her. "Hey Sissy, what's up?" Cat answered.

"Do you have a minute?" Kris asked.

"Of course I do, what do you need? You actually sound upset."

"Elaine quit her practice, and I feel like I am sinking.

"Are you still seeing Shelby?"

"Yes, but it just isn't the same. I have this letter that I wrote to the department about what happened, and I read them to Shelby and just have to decide if I am going to send them."

"Well, what is the worst that can happen if you send them?" She asked as the social worker/big sister mode kicked in.

"The worst that can happen is they completely ignore it and throw the letters away," Kris responded.

"So then you are prepared to not hear anything back at all. You know how police departments work, and how they cover for each other. What will you be out?" Cat asked.

"The cost of the paper and stamps."

"Exactly. I think you already know what your decision is then Sissy."

"Thanks big sister."

"Of course. Hey, what did you say the name of that one officer was?"

"I didn't and I won't, but good try. How are my nephews doing? I talked to Alex once since he moved to Chicago, and Joseph texts me from time to time, but that is about it."

"Alex is doing good, loving Chicago, and Joseph has been busy as can be with school and theater stuff," Cat replied.

They talked for a few more minutes about things going on at home and then hung up with the promise that Kris would keep

Cat updated on what she was doing. She also tried to get the name of her assailants out of Kris a couple more times but to no avail. While Kris was pretty sure Cat had been joking back in February, she was also sure that Cat would find a way to make the two officers lives a living hell without doing physical harm. But this was all for Kris to handle at this point. She had still not read the letter to Tony. He was now seeing his own therapist, but there was quite a bit of tension between them again and it stemmed from the hurt of the affairs Tony had over the last few years. She did not feel comfortable sharing the details of the letter with him at this point and wasn't sure she ever would. She was tired of feeling hurt and being hurt by the men in her life. The betrayals seemed to just keep coming, and she often wondered what she'd done in a past life to deserve it all. Kris knew that at some point she was going to have to share the letter with him, especially when she sent it to the people she addressed it to. She was going to have to clue him in as to what was going on with the situation.

A couple of weeks later, when Tony came home from work, she was sitting at the table making out the grocery list. As he came into the kitchen, he put his lunch containers in the sink, and placed his hand on her shoulder squeezing it gently. "How was your day?" he asked.

"It wasn't horrible. I am going to go have lunch with the guys before my appointment with Shelby this week if you don't mind," Kris said.

"Not at all, tell them I said hello. Is Clint going to be there too?"

"I think so. It will be nice to see them. I haven't seen Clint since he graduated." While attending school up in Richmond, Kris had made friends with Clint in some of her Anthropology classes, and they took Spanish classes together where they met Simon and eventually met Simon's partner Brandon. Kris loved going up there and hanging out with Simon and Brandon and occasionally Clint was able to meet them, as long as he had someone to watch his son.

"Tony, can you sit down for a minute?"

"Is everything okay?" he asked.

Kris pulled the letter out from under the grocery list and slid it over to him. "I want you to read this. I have every intention at this point in sending it to everyone it is addressed to, and think it is important that you know the content. I don't know what is going to happen once they get it, but I will be sending it certified--that way I know it was received. The only thing I ask is that you do not throw any of this in my face and don't use it as a reason to be 'cautious' with me. There is a difference in what those two did to me and the physical aspect of our marriage, and I know what it is." He took the letter and sat over on the couch while she continued with the list and menu planning for the next couple of weeks. After a few minutes, he came over to her and quietly grabbed her hand, stood her up, and pulled her into his arms. "I am so sorry Kris. I don't have any other words other than I am sorry that this happened to you. I will say that I am behind you in whatever you decide to do with this and will be there every step of the way. I do have one question for you though."

"What's that?" she replied.

"Does your dad know about this?"

"Not yet, and I am not sure if I will tell him. Mom knows and so do Cat and Lilly. I shared it with a couple of friends too but as far as family just Mom and my sisters."

"I think it would be best if your dad didn't know. You know what his reaction is going to be," Tony said .

"Yeah I know. Pretty much the same as Cat's. She is out for blood, and I am sure Dad's reaction will be even more intense."

Kris had some serious concerns about her father learning of this; she knew he would want to kill them. No questions asked, he would be ready to shed blood and go to prison because one of his baby girls was hurt. While it was admirable, it was also a little annoying seeing as how any man that he felt "wronged" his daughters was fair game. It is almost as though they were not allowed to grow up or experience the pains in life. Kris' mom was more in the path of the "survivor's guilt." She wanted to know why she couldn't protect her daughter, what she could have done differently, etc. Nothing. There was nothing that could have been done differently in any situation that Kris had gone through. Not the abuse as a child, not the incident in front of her house in high school, not the heartbreaks through dating, and surely not this. Kris understood her mom just wanted to help, and she wanted to take some of that pain away from her baby, but the best thing any of her family or friends could do was be supportive and lend a shoulder or an ear when she needed it.

The following day, Kris got on the internet and looked up the address to the police department and addressed the envelopes. While she was out running other errands, she stopped by the post office and mailed three copies of the letter, all certified and requesting a signature to ensure receipt of delivery. What happened to the letters after that was beyond her control. She could not make any of them read the letters or respond to them, but it sure did feel good to put the information out there and let them know that their department and the officers were not as wholesome or blameless as they made them out to be--for their public image. A weight had been lifted off of Kris' shoulders, and she could feel some of the tension leave her body. That night she slept better than she had in a long time. Tony wrapped his arms around her, and she peacefully fell asleep listening to his heart beating.

CHAPTER FIVE

Life seemed to continue as a somewhat normal pace for the next few days. She went up to Richmond for an appointment with Shelby and met her friends, Simon, and Brandon, for lunch. Clint was unable to make it this time and said to send his apologies but would meet them all soon. They met over at a small café on the corner of Cary and Cherry Streets. It was a place they frequented often during school, and Kris had become friends with one of the waitresses, Audra Wooldridge. Audra had helped Kris through the last affair Tony had, as well as offered a place to go whenever she needed time away. Kris had met Audra one day after Audra was finishing her shift, and they walked through the Oregon Hill area of Richmond talking while Kris cried a lot trying to process the last affair. Now as she was sitting there waiting for the guys, Audra sat down while it was slow and asked Kris, "So what's going on with you? You look pretty well rested compared to the last time I saw you."

"I am," Kris replied. "Remember the letters I told you I wrote? Well I sent them off yesterday, and I finally got some sleep. It doesn't happen often but I will take it when it comes."

"I am so glad to hear that Kris. I know things have not been going very well for you the last year or so. What does Shelby have to say about it?"

"I have not seen her since I sent them. My appointment is this afternoon, and I am waiting for the guys to get here for lunch."

"You want a Coke or something else?"

"Actually if I could get some water and then a Malibu and Pineapple juice that would be great. I have plenty of time before my appointment, and will have some food on my stomach."

"I've got it, and here come the guys."

Simon and Brandon walked in, and Audra had their drinks ready with Kris'. They had all been coming there so frequently over the years that Audra had their orders down pat. She didn't even have to ask Simon how he wanted his salad. "Clint isn't going to make it this time. His son is sick, and he had to take him to the doctor." Kris informed the guys. The three of them ordered and sat there shooting the breeze, Audra joining the conversation when she could talk between customers.

"You know Audra, it would be easier to have a conversation if all of these people would stop coming in to eat," Brandon said to her.

"I know right. How rude of them? This is like watching a soap opera every couple of years trying to pick up on the conversation."

They all laughed and Simon told her, "Don't worry, we are saving all the good gossip for you."

Audra looked at Kris and said, "You can fill them in on what I already know, and that way I don't miss anything." She said laughing. Kris told them about sending the letters out the previous day. They already knew the content of them, since she sent Brandon a copy so he could do any editing that needed to be done as far as grammar and spelling was concerned. At the time, he informed her he had to read it three or four times to make it all the way through. "Do you know how hard it is to read something when you are sobbing?" he had asked her after reading it.

They sat there for another hour or so and went to the food cart on campus to get a drink before Kris had to drive the few blocks to Shelby's office. Brandon and Simon had to get back to work so they left after getting their drinks and while she was waiting for hers, Kris' phone chirped. When it went off, it played a ringtone specific to Elaine's number. "Hello."

"Kris, its Elaine."

"I know, your ringtone is still programed into my phone. What's up?"

"I wanted to let you know that I am starting back up June 1, and if you wanted to come back and see me I can get you back in the schedule."

"'That would be fine. A lot has happened over the period of time you've been gone."

"Fantastic, I can't wait to hear about what is going on. I have to be honest with you, I didn't think you would want to come back after our last appointment. You appeared to be pretty mad," Elaine said cautiously.

"I wasn't mad Elaine, I was shocked and hurt by what I perceived to be abandonment. You will understand that more when I see you." They set the appointment, and Kris went up to Shelby's office.

Kris sat down and told Shelby about sending the letters off to the department. They processed the content of the letters and did some EMDR work with it because Kris began getting worked up. Shelby gave Kris some tools to work through the feelings she was having and then talked a little bit about Elaine's return. A small part of Kris had still felt betrayed by Elaine, but on a bigger level knew it had absolutely nothing to do with her. Everyone has their own "stuff" to handle, and it was unavoidable for Elaine. Kris was quite sure it would be the topic of discussion at least once in the process of catching up. Kris drove home feeling lighter than she had in quite some time, but she couldn't help but think about the letters and what the reaction would be when they made it to their destinations. She really was not expecting much, because after all they were cops, and cops protected each other.

A week later, Kris was outside picking tomatoes and herbs from the garden, and then she lit the grill for dinner. Kris heard the doorbell ring, and Tony called for her. "Kris, you have a registered letter you need to sign for." Kris' heart started pounding, and she knew that it was a response to her letters, but she was not expecting it to be from the department that had sent it. When she signed for the letter, she sat down at the kitchen table and took a deep breath before she opened it. She was shaking so badly that she could barely hold the letter in her hand. Tony came up behind her and rubbed her shoulders, leaned down and kissed her on the top of the head and said, "You did the hardest part of this when you sent it. You've got this babe." She opened the letter, which was not from any of the divisions she had sent hers to, but from the Sex Crimes Unit of the St. Louis Police Department. "Dear Mrs. Parker, I am in receipt of your letter describing the incident which occurred while you were working for the St. Louis Police Department." The letter went on to say that the sergeant in charge of the unit stated he would like to hear from Kris when she was ready, and they could discuss the incident and her options pertaining to it. When she finished reading the letter, she put it down, hands still shaking and just started sobbing. Tony stood next to her, pulled her closer, and as he did, she buried her face into his chest and sobbed. Her eyes were nearly dried shut with all-consuming tears.

They didn't speak for quite some time but when she was ready, she wiped the tears from her face and eyes and said to Tony, "They want to do something about it. The sergeant wants me to call him so we can talk about my options. They believed me Tony, and they didn't ignore it. I truly thought they would just brush this aside, but they didn't."

Tony held on to her, tears in his own eyes, and said, "I am behind you no matter what happens. When you need me to stand back I will, when you need me right there, I will be there. I am so sorry that this happened to you and that I cannot do something about it. This is all for you to handle, but I am here for you no matter what. I admire the strength it took to write that letter and then to send it. I don't think I have met anyone with that kind of strength and courage." He hugged her tightly, pulled back and looked at her with a sly grin and said, "Now, where's my dinner?" She gave him a playful slap on the arm, and they both started laughing.

June 2013

Kris sat down at her computer and started playing games on a social media sight when she saw a notification on her sister Cat's page. One of her friends commented on a photo. When Kris looked at the name, she thought to herself, surely this isn't the same person I went to the Academy with? She called Cat and left her a message letting her know it wasn't urgent but to call her when she got the chance. Later that evening Cat called her and when she answered the phone, she asked, "Hey Sissy, what's up?"

"Hey Cat, I wanted to ask you about someone on your friends list. The Ronnie Lowell that commented on your page, is she by any chance a St. Louis Police officer? I cannot see her page yet."

"Yes. Why do you ask?"

"How do you know her?" Kris asked.

"She was at a training that I attended and I see her from time to time when I go out with friends from the court. She is working in the homicide division in St. Louis."

"I think I graduated with her from the police academy." Kris replied.

"I will be sure to ask her when I see her. She obviously works different hours, but on occasion I will see her. Anything else going on?"

"Yes, Elaine came back to her practice and I will be seeing her in a couple of days."

"Are you still planning on coming home for Mom and Dad's birthday?" Cat asked.

"Of course, just let me know what else I need to do to help. I will do as much as I can from here."

"Have you heard anything else from the department?"

Kris told her that she had an appointment to meet with a detective when she came home and that she was still unsure if she was going to file formal charges. "It is different being on the other side of this situation. I was always nervous when I went to court, but this is completely different knowing I am going to be on the other side."

"It will be okay sister. Take someone with you just to be there when you finish."

"Kate and Lilly are going with me, and then we are headed to lunch after that." Lilly is the youngest sister to Cat and Kris, and Kate

63

and Kris had been friends since middle school meeting through Girl Scouts.

They talked a few more minutes and then said their goodbyes. Two days later, Kris took the drive up to Richmond and walked the stairs to Elaine's office. She waited a few minutes before Elaine came in to get her and when they walked back to her office, Kris hadn't completely sat down when Elaine said, "So first things first, I want to hear exactly what you were feeling that day I told you I had to leave the practice for a while."

"First thing was I hoped everything was okay with you and your family, next I was really pissed off and hurt. I felt like I had been betrayed on some levels and wanted to tell you to fuck off. I also know that everyone goes through things that cannot be helped, but I think I would have been better off had you gotten out of that chair and punched me in the face. It may have been less devastating at the time considering what I had just done that week."

Elaine looked at her with a quizzical expression and asked, "What is it you did that week? I don't have anything of significance in my notes."

Kris handed over a copy of the letter and as Elaine started to read it, she looked up and said, "Oh, wow. Oh my God, I just now noticed the date. Did you have this with you that day?"

"Yes I did and had every intention of reading it aloud to you that day."

"Would you be willing to read it out loud now? You have never shared the details with me about this, just that it happened and when it happened. I am assuming the details are in here?" Elaine asked.

"They are and yes, I can read it to you." Kris proceeded to read the letter to Elaine but not without tears, having to take several deep breaths while trying to control her anger. When she finished reading the letter, the tears flooded out as Elaine pointed out the sadness that surfaced when Kris was reading a portion describing the true reason she left the department and that realization 16 years later.

As she dried her face and started to calm down a bit, Kris looked at Elaine and said, "I loved that job Elaine. I loved it, and I was good at it. It was one of the few times I felt good about who I am as a person and those mother fuckers took it from me and never gave me the chance to know why. There are times right now where I would give up everything I have right now to be back in that uniform. I fought so hard to be there, and they took that from me. They took a part of me that I will never get back." The tears started pouring out again, only this time they were flooding out of pure anger and rage.

"You know Kris, it is okay to let this all go. Just let it out however you need to. Sometimes I grab a pillow and just scream into it."

"No way. I can't do that."

"And why not? Are you afraid it will shock me or make me leave the room? This is the safest place, next to your house, that you could do this."

"I am afraid other people in this building will hear it and think I have really lost it."

"Nobody will hear you, I promise," Elaine reassured her.

After a couple of minutes, Kris put the pillow up to her face and just screamed. She screamed until it was physically exhausting, and she felt like she was going to pass out. When she looked up from the pillow, Elaine waited and when she felt like Kris was ready, began to speak again. "How did that feel?"

"Like I was going to pass out, but it felt good. I am sure there is more in there at this point that just isn't ready to come out."

Elaine smiled and said, "I am sure there is, and you are welcome to let it out in here any time you need. So tell me, what you are going to do with the letter?"

"Oh, I already sent it and heard back from them." Kris told her.

"Oh wow. You have been busy in my absence, haven't you? What did they say?" Kris conveyed the content of the letter and the conversation she had with the sergeant in charge of the Sex Crimes Unit with the department.

"I am going to be going home in July for my parents' birthdays and have made arrangements to meet with a detective to discuss what options I have are as far as filing charges. He assured me that this would be investigated to its fullest extent. They are also going to provide me with a Sexual Assault Advocate while they talk to me."

"How do you feel about all of this?"

"It is scary but at the same time I am feeling a sense of relief and confusion all at once."

"What is the confusion part of it?" Elaine asked.

"I still cannot come up with that other officer's name, and it is making me crazy. I am always so good with names and the kicker part is, I remember having a conversation with this guy a few years ago when I was at a friend's house on New Year's Eve. She knew him through a mutual friend, and when she was talking to him she asked me 'Kris, do you remember _____?' and said his full name. I knew who it was and that he was associated with Mack. Hell, I didn't remember anything about that incident then either. I also remember that it wasn't too long after that, that I lost contact with her. She never returned phone calls, emails and I got a final email telling me how busy she was with life in general, but I think something else was going on."

"Well you know Shelby and I are both here if you need anything. We can talk more about it next time I see you. We have a couple of appointments before you go out of town to process all of this."

Kris drove home, windows down, and music up loud. Sometimes she really enjoyed the solitude of the drive and found herself getting lost in its seclusion. Tony had warned her a couple of times to pay more attention to where she was in case something happened, and she needed to let someone know exactly where she was. There were many times he would call her and ask where she was in her drive and the common answer was "I don't know, on 64 somewhere." Today was no different and she had to be conscience of the fact that she needed to look at the mile markers on the highway. Elaine had instructed her to journal anything she was feeling as she processed all of the information, but she was hesitant to do so for fear of what else was going to come out. The information she had been processing was still difficult to handle, and she was still having nightmares. They weren't nearly as frequent as they had been in the past, but once in a while they would pop through. Kris still wished the name of that second officer would unveil itself.

July/August, 2013

The next few weeks went by relatively normal. Kris and Tony celebrated their 15th wedding anniversary in Richmond. Tony had reserved a room, and they met with Simon and Brandon for dinner at a Mexican restaurant in Cary Town. Then the following day they went to Maymont Park and walked the entire park. It was a very nice few days before Kris prepared for her drive back to St. Louis. Going back there had always been preceded by stress, arguments with Tony, and lots of tension when she was there. This time there had not been any arguments, and the stress felt much different. It was more of a nervousness, an anxiousness. Tony walked into the bedroom where Kris was packing up some of her clothing and said, "I can fly out there and go with you to the police department if you want and then stay for your mom's and dad's birthday party."

"No, I don't want you to use what little leave time you do have. Then you won't have any time off at Christmas and will end up with no paycheck."

"Well if you change your mind you just say the word, and I will be there for you. Even if I just have to fly out to go to the department with you I will. I know I haven't said much about this, but I want you to know how much I admire what you are doing. This is not an easy thing to do, and you have been handling it all so well. You are so strong. I don't know that I could be that strong with something like this. I wish I could do more for you."

"Just listening and holding me is enough right now," Kris replied.

"Well, whatever happens after this, I will be there. I will save up all the time necessary so you do not have to do this alone anymore.

I have to tell you, though, I am with your dad on this one. Those assholes need to die."

"Tony, while you are both probably right, it doesn't help me at all to hear this. Talk amongst yourselves because when you are saying this, and this is a collective 'you' not just specifically aimed at you, I am hearing 'you didn't do enough to help yourself.' I know that isn't really what you are all saying, but I already feel like shit about this right now."

"I'm sorry babe. You are right, and I need to think about what you are going through more and be there for you." He hugged Kris and held her tight.

As Kris made her way across Interstate 64 to St. Louis, she did a lot of thinking. She was still hung up on the fact that she could not remember the name of the other officer who had participated in such a horrific event. Despite the conversations with Elaine, she still could not help but blame herself either. When Elaine asked her why she felt it was her fault, Kris responded, "I was entrusted by the City of St. Louis and the State of Missouri to protect its citizens, and I couldn't even protect myself. How in the hell do I come to terms with that? I know that I did not choose this to happen to me, but I did choose to go out and have a couple of drinks after work. I shouldn't have gone out." Kris remembers the look on Elaine's face when she said that. While she was trying to maintain her professionalism, Kris could hear the frustration in her voice when she responded. "Are you serious? Let me ask you this…did you CHOOSE for them to drug your drink, because based on your description, I would lay odds on that being what happened. And did you CHOOSE for them to rape you repeatedly for hours and then either dump you off at your car to drive home, still in a drugged state, or at your house after one of them drove your car home? Did you CHOOSE these things Kris?"

Kris had finally responded after she had finished crying and could actually do so. "Of course I didn't choose for that to all happen."

"Exactly. You may have well have said that you were asking for it. You weren't, Kris, and you had every right to expect that they were going to do exactly as they said they would do and take you home after having a couple of drinks--without taking the time to rape you. You had no reason NOT to trust them to treat you any differently. These were co-workers and friends, and there was nothing to indicate they were anything else. Am I wrong in that assessment?"

"Not at all. You know that I had been having a physical relationship with Mack already. I just still don't understand why he would do that to me? There is a very big part of me who KNOWS there is nothing I could have done differently or to even stop what happened. I truly believe it was planned out from the beginning and if it didn't happen on that day, it would have happened on another day. There is also that part of me who feels all this guilt that isn't even mine." Kris said.

"I understand Kris, but it is going to take some time before you fully understand it, and that's okay too. That comes with the healing, and that in itself has no timeline or directions on how to get there. It is different for everyone, and I am sorry to be the bearer of bad news, but in all the books I have read studying this profession, nobody gave me a manual to hand out to every client on the exact way to heal." Kris laughed a little, knowing that Elaine was right.

The drive was relatively uneventful—Kris making her normal stops along the way, including the hotel stay overnight. It was about 14 hours to St. Louis and then another hour to her parents' house the St. Louis city limits. Despite the heat in places, she rode with the windows down and the music turned up loud--enough to hear it over the blowing wind. The solitude was doing some good, and as she had laid in the bed at the hotel, she cried some more. The tears came easily and frequently. She was feeling quite a bit of anger about this as much as she was feeling the hurt. She loved her job with the department and really missed it. She thought about how in a matter of hours, it was all taken from her and she never even knew why. Kris thought about Wanda and Andrew and wanted so badly to talk to them and explain why she left, that she now knew the real reason she was feeling the way she was. She had no way of getting in touch with them. She knew that Wanda had retired a few years earlier and was actually afraid to call anyone at the department to get in touch with Andrew. Who really knew what was going on with that department? Kris remembers what a rumor mill it could be, and she was curious as to who already knew about her letters and their content. Kris was trying to stay focused on the other purpose of her trip, and that was for her parents' 70th birthdays. She, Cat, and Lilly were planning a surprise party for them, and Kris wanted to jump in and help with anything she could from there. She had not been able to do much due to her physical distance from everyone, but now she could jump in with both feet. Her appointment with the police department was the week after the party and for all her parents knew, she was coming home for the appointment.

A couple of hours later as Kris approached the city limits of St. Louis, she called her friend and former roommate Lynn. Lynn worked in the city for the local power company, and they had planned on going to lunch when Kris arrived. Kris picked up Lynn at work, and the headed toward lunch. "How are doing you doing with all of this?" Lynn asked.

"I am nervous as hell, Lynn. It is a different animal all together knowing that I am going to be sitting on the other side of that interview table."

"Kris, I am so sorry this happened to you. I wish I would have known. I don't know what I would have done, but damn. I don't ever remember meeting Mack. Did he ever come over to the apartment?"

"Yes he was there, but now that I think about it, he always made sure you were never there. He made sure you didn't know who he was. As far as not knowing, don't feel bad. Obviously I didn't have a clue either."

"Well if you need anything Kris, I am here for you. This is not going to be an easy road, and I am sure you are going to have to repeat this over several times before it is all said and done. Know that you have a lot of support beside you, and now that we know about this you won't have to do it alone anymore," Lynn said.

"Thanks Lynn. It means a lot to me knowing that I have so many people in my corner."

"Exactly, and if all else fails we can just make sure they disappear, never to be heard from again," She said as she laughed.

Kris laughed along with her and replied, "Yeah, I am beginning to think that list is a little longer than the ones in my corner."

"No," Lynn said, "I would be willing to bet it is the same exact number of people ."

"I will take that bet," Kris responded. The remainder of the lunch was spent catching up on events since the last time they talked on the phone. Kris took Lynn back to work and then drove the forty-five minutes to her parents' house in Wentzville.

The next few days revolved around party planning and buying necessary last minute items. At one point Kris and her mom had gone to the local wholesale club and when Kris offered to buy a beef brisket for dinner (knowing it was for the party, not a family dinner), her mom insisted she was not going to pay for food that the family was going to be eating. "How many do you think we need Kris?" her mom asked.

"We better get two, even as big as they are, because I am sure Cat will want to take some home to Joe since he is working. Plus I think she could eat a brisket all on her own," Kris said laughing. The briskets were pretty large, but they were expecting over 50 people. Even though there was going to be other meat, they didn't want to chance running out of food. The guests were all bringing side dishes as well. Cat already had the day planned for their parents with a Scavenger hunt where they had to be at certain events at specific times and then back home for the "family dinner" at a set time too. All three of them were so excited about the event. Lilly and her husband arranged a slide show of pictures from the time their parents were babies to the present—70 years of photos. The party had gone off without a hitch, and Kris' mom and dad were so excited and surprised. At one point Cat and Lilly came upstairs and asked Kris for the third brisket. "We only had the two big ones. Why?"

The other two looked at each other and Joan said, "We better get down there and get some before it is gone."

"What happened to the chicken and pork?" Kris asked.

Cat replied, "Oh it is still there, but the brisket is almost all gone." The two ran downstairs before Kris could say anything else, and Kris' nephew was not far behind them.

"I will be back Aunt Kisstine, (the name stuck through both nephews no matter how old they were) I have to get food before my mom and Aunt Lilly take it all." Kris laughed as they all heaped beef onto their plates and hid them so nobody else could steal it. Kris didn't find out until later that night that neither of her parents got some of the brisket. "You know Mom," Kris said to her, "The worst part is, YOU paid for them."

CHAPTER SIX

The next couple of days following the party and leading up to the appointment with the police department, Kris kept herself distracted. Her sister Lilly took her to a place in St. Louis County so she could have Reiki done. It was the first time she had ever had a complete Reiki session done in a quiet setting. She did have a woman in the Detroit airport do it to help get rid of a migraine, but it was just a short session.

When Kris had it done in the airport, she wasn't quite sure what it was, and before she went, Lilly explained to her: Reiki is a Japanese alternative medicine. It is a form of energy healing where the person giving the Reiki uses their hands and basically transfers healing energy to the recipient. This was quite intensive, and Kris could feel the heaviness inside her body lifting. The Reiki practitioner told Kris the things that she could 'see' through her third eye during the session, and everything she had told Kris she 'saw' and felt was very connected to her current situation. Kris had filled her in on the basics of what happened, because she felt just like with her therapy, someone cannot help fix or sort issues out if information is missing. Kris had not, however, mentioned Andrew to her and when the session was over she described his appearance in detail to Kris. Kris knew then, she needed to find out where both Andrew and Wanda were. On the way home from Reiki, Kris did a quick check in with Elaine to make sure they still had a phone appointment for the time following her interview with the detective. After a brief chat with Elaine, Kris called Kate to make sure she was still taking her down to the downtown headquarters. Lilly planned on meeting them there, and then the three were going to lunch afterwards. Both of her parents offered to drive her, but there was absolutely no part this that she wanted her parents to be exposed to. It was bad enough they had to know the basics, but she knew they would just sit there and stew, especially her dad. He was still on a tear and constantly mumbling about how they needed to be dead.

Both he and her sister Cat were trying their best to get Kris to slip up and give them Mack's name. Kris was on to them and everything they tried ultimately failed.

Kate picked Kris up the following morning around 9 am. They drove down to the City of St. Louis and met up with Kris' sister Lilly. Before they walked into the headquarters building, Lilly looked at her older sister and said, "I just want to let you know that no matter what happens I am so proud of you big seeester. This is not an easy thing, and you are so brave. If you wanted to change your mind, nobody would fault you for it or think badly of you."

Tears started to form in Kris' eyes, and she told Lilly, "I've got this. I have to say though, I don't think I could do this if you and Kate were not here." Kris hugged them both and the three of them walked in.

Kris noticed how much had changed since she left. There was now a long desk in front of the elevators leading up to the different divisions where visitors had to sign in and go through a metal detector. When Kris walked up to the desk, she had to list who she was there to see and what division. She felt a little bit embarrassed when she had to write down that she was there to talk to a detective in the Sex Crimes Unit. Jesus, she thought, how in the hell did this happen? It felt a little like she was someone else, and it wasn't really her that was getting ready to do this. She closed her eyes for just a moment, hoping Lilly and Kate did not notice, because she knew this feeling. She remembered that feeling of being outside of herself pertaining to this incident, and she did not want to "blank out" like she had done so many times in the recent past. She could hear Elaine's voice in her head, reminding her to be present in that moment and to feel her feet on the floor and relax. Every muscle in her body was tense.

A few moments later, Detective Ken Pollack exited the elevator, approached the desk looking at her and said, "Kris Parker?"

"Yes sir."

"I'm Detective Pollack. Come on up, and we can get started."

"Is it okay if my sister and friend come up and wait for me?"

"Not a problem at all. The Sexual Assault Advocate is on her way, so they can wait with you until she arrives. After that, obviously they will have to leave the room."

"Of course, I understand." Kris replied. She remembered enough that having anyone else in the interview room could compromise the integrity of the investigation. The elevator ride to the fourth floor was quiet and when they stepped off and started walking down the hall, a flood of memories came back into her head. Again the tears started and this time, Kate noticed because Kris felt her put a hand on Kris' shoulder and slightly rub it as if to say, you are going to be okay. Kris remembered the smells, the darkness of the hallways and spending many hours assisting some of the divisions, especially Homicide, with supplemental information for reports.

They walked into the Sex Crimes Division and wound through desks and offices to reach a large conference room in the back of the division. Kris, Lilly, and Kate sat down and Detective Pollack asked, "Can I get anyone something to drink?" They all replied that they did not need anything. "I am going to check to see where the advocate is. She should be here pretty soon," he said.

"Thank you" Kris replied. Kate and Lilly, sat there making small talk with Kris until the detective returned with the SAA.

When he did, Kate and Lilly stood up and Kate said, "We will be right outside the door. If you need anything, don't you hesitate to come get us."

"Thanks Kate."

The sexual assault advocate introduced herself as Sydney and explained her role and what she could do for Kris during the process. Kris could feel her heart rate start to pick up and was doing her best to maintain her composure. Sydney sat next to Kris, and Detective Pollack sat across from Kris at the large table. The feeling was worse than Kris thought. It was so different being the person interviewed than the one conducting the interview. As she looked at the detective, she couldn't help but think, I wonder how old you were when all this shit went down, or if you were even born yet? He was young, with dark hair, and a very serious demeanor. Kris' head was swimming, and staying in the present was a difficult struggle. She felt like she was actually fighting both her mind and her body from completely disassociating at this point. Now she knew what many others felt like when they were sitting on this side of the table. Witness, victim, or suspect, she imagined having to tell their "story" to a police officer had to be nerve wracking, and she most assuredly felt their pain in that moment.

Detective Pollack opened his binder and wrote the date, time, and the name of everyone in the room. He began by asking Kris questions of pedigree and other basic information that would be included in the report. He pulled out the copy of the letter that Kris had originally sent to everyone in April. "As you can see, I have a copy of the letter, which is quite detailed, but I still need to hear you tell me what happened. If you don't remember something, don't force the information because if you remember later we can always add it into a supplemental report. My first question is: What made you decide to come talk to us? It said in your letter that you were not sure about pressing charges or even talking to us."

"When the sergeant responded, I wasn't sure what I wanted to do, but he explained to me that we could just have a conversation to start and I could decide from there how far I wanted to go with this," Kris replied.

"Okay. Let me make you aware that I do not know Mack Parkins personally and never worked with him. I don't know anything about him other than I know he has relatives who were officers in the past and that Mack no longer works for the department. Why don't you tell me what you can recall? Actually, do you remember what time of year it was? I know you said in the letter that you were unsure. Is that still the case?"

"Yes. I am still unsure, but it may have been in the summer. I remember sitting in Mack's little pickup truck in front of the grocery store and just feeling so hot. I don't know if it was hot air blowing on me from the vent, or if it were just still hot inside the car from the outside temperature."

"What type of vehicle did he drive?"

"I don't remember the make, but it was a small black pickup with a camper shell on the back. On the back bumper was a sticker that read 'Don't Mess with Texas,'" she replied.

Kris continued on with the narrative and only brief interruptions by Detective Pollack asking questions or clarifying what she was saying. She was talking about having arrived at the bar, CODE 40, which was owned by two former police officers from the city. She told the detective about having had a drink, some food, and ordering a second drink. "I let my second drink get watered down, because I knew I had to work that night and was starting to get really tired. I finished the food to help absorb what I already drank."

"Do you remember what you were drinking?" he asked.

"It may have been a Tequila Sunrise or rum and Coke. I remember those being my drinks of choice at that time."

"Okay."

"At some point after ordering my second drink I had to use the ladies room, so I left my keys and badge case on the bar, and asked Mack to watch them when I went to the restroom. He said he would watch them and not to worry. I still had my gun on me though."

"Mrs. Parker, do you remember where everyone was sitting?"

"Yes. We were at the end of the bar closest to the restrooms, but still towards the middle of the bar, if that makes sense."

"It does. Do you remember where they were sitting in relation to where you were?" he asked.

"There was nobody on my left, Mack was to my right and the other guy was on Mack's right."

"The other guy being the one you think was being trained by Mack and the other person who was involved in the incident?"

"Yes."

"I'm sorry, please continue." Detective Pollack said.

"I came back from the restroom and as I sat down I saw a new drink sitting on the bar at the place I was sitting. I said something to Mack about it, and he told me he bought it for me because my other one was watered down."

"Was it the same kind of drink you had the first time?"

"Yes, but it tasted really weird," she answered.

"What do you mean by 'weird?'"

"It was definitely stronger, and it tasted really bitter. It had a really funny taste to it. I told Mack I didn't want to drink it because I had to go home and get some sleep before I went to work that night. He told me not to worry; he would give me a ride home, and everyone had to work that night. It was at this point I noticed my keys missing from on top of my badge case."

The tears started flowing quite steadily at this point, and she felt Sydney's hand on her arm helping her to calm down a little. Kris had, up to this point, maintained her composure despite the original struggle to stay in the present. When she started talking to the detective, she did what any cop would do and that was to take the emotion out of the situation. It had worked well up to this point. Having to tell this in person was much more difficult than she thought. It was starting to hit her and she could no longer keep the emotions and feelings at bay. "Mrs. Parker, I know this is difficult, but could you tell me what happened when you left the bar? Again I have all of this information in front of me but I need to hear it from you as well."

"I wanted to drive myself home, but Mack insisted he would give me a ride and that I was too drunk to drive."

"How did you feel at that point?" he asked.

"I was feeling quite intoxicated at the time and wasn't really sure why because I had only had what amounted to two drinks. I remember attributing it to being really tired since we had just all come off the night shift." Kris took a deep breath because she could feel herself starting to disappear. She could feel the start of the disassociation behind her eyes because they were starting to hurt, the same way her eyes hurt in the past when she began to disassociate.

"I had asked Mack several times where my keys were and he told me not to worry about them, that he would take care of me. He wouldn't give me my keys so I finally told him to just take me home," she continued. "The three of us got into Mack's truck..."

"Do you remember where you were sitting?" Detective Pollack interrupted.

"I was between Mack and the other guy," she replied. He continued to make notes as she talked and it was actually making her nervous for some reason. It may have been because she could not see what he was writing and this was such a foreign concept for her to be on this side of the interview table. "He..."

"Mack?"

"Yes, Mack. Mack told me he had to stop by the grocery store on the way home to pick up some stuff for dinner that his wife asked him to get. When we pulled into the parking lot, he told me to stay in the truck. I think I was alone but honestly don't remember. By this time I could barely keep my head up and just wanted to go home. I remember Mack had a brown paper bag in his hands, and he and the other guy were laughing in the truck."

Kris was still having problems fighting the tears and the desire to just give in to the disassociation. Sydney had not said much more than words of reassurance and encouragement, telling Kris how good she was doing and helping her stay calm. "We drove away from the store, and then he turned in the opposite direction from my home. I asked him why he was going in the other direction, and he told me because he was taking the other guy back to his car; they had gone to the bar together. When we arrived at Mack's house..."

"Is this the first time you had ever been to his house? I only ask because in your letter you stated that you had already been having a physical relationship with him."

"Yes, it was the first time I had ever been to his house. He was married, so anything that took place was at my apartment." More writing. "When we got to Mack's house, he said he wanted to have a beer before he took me home and asked the other officer if he wanted one too. Despite not wanting to be there, I went in. He was my only way home. I couldn't even call my roommate at this point because I had no clue where I was, and she was at work."

"What happened after you went inside?" The detective asked.

"When we got inside, he pulled beer out of the paper bag and asked the other officer if he wanted a beer. I told him I really just wanted to get home, but he told me that they wanted to have a beer first, and I should just relax. Mack said he would get me home in enough time for me to get sleep before my shift. I could barely stand, but I had to use the restroom so I asked where it was and he gave me directions. I put my weapon, and badge case on the mantel of the fireplace and struggled to get to the bathroom. When I came out I could hear the magazine being ejected from one of the handguns. As I came around the corner I realized it was mine and Mack was ejecting the magazine and the round in the chamber."

Kris struggled to maintain composure at this point, because she knew that she was going to have to finish telling what happened and in full detail. She was sobbing by this point and could barely breathe. The detective stopped asking questions and writing, and he waited for her to be able to speak again. Sydney rubbed the back of Kris' shoulder and told her she was doing well—to take her time. Kris took a deep breath and finished telling Detective Pollack what had transpired from the point of seeing and hearing the round leave her weapon until she woke up later that night to get ready for work. He asked if she remembered anything they had said, and at the time she could not remember everything. She had put that information in her journal, but of course she wasn't reading from her journal and was in a completely different state of mind then and now. She told him that the atmosphere was that of a frat house party, that they were laughing; joking and high-fiving each other as they took turns raping her. She explained she did not know how she really made it home, just that when she woke up that night to get ready for work her car was parked out in front of her apartment.

The interview took place for another 15 to 20 minutes. Before he left the room, Detective Pollack handed her a business card and said, "Mrs. Parker, if you remember anything else please give me a call and we will add it to the report, especially if you remember the name of the other officer. Do you think you would be able to identify him in a photo array?"

"Yes, I think I could."

"Are you sure that Mack was his training officer and that he was new to the department?"

"I am pretty sure Mack was his F.T.O., but it is possible he just rode with him a few times. I do know that he was fairly new, only out of the academy, maybe a month or so."

"Okay, I will see what I can find out and be in touch with you. When are you leaving to go back to Virginia? I am hoping we can get some photos together before that for you to look at and to talk with the circuit attorney." Kris let him know when she was leaving and that she would make sure she was available to talk to the circuit attorney if it became necessary. When he left the room she laid her head on her arms and sobbed. She was exhausted and just wanted to leave. After she pulled herself together, Sydney walked her, Lilly, and Kate to the elevator and back to the front door. When they left, they went to a sushi place on Washington Avenue to relax and step back from what had just taken place.

Kate and Kris drove back to Kris' parents' house, and Kris picked a few things up to take to Kate's house. She was going to follow Kate back to her house and have dinner and some wine out there. Kate and her husband lived a little further out from her mom and dad's house, and Kris loved to be there to just relax and escape. She and Kate picked up some food to snack on and a couple of bottles of wine. They were sitting out on the deck, listening to the sounds of crickets and frogs, watching the sun lower over the pasture and horses. "How are you doing girl?" Kate asked.

"I am doing okay I think. I just really wish I could remember the name of that other officer. It is going to make me crazy, well crazier than what I already am," she said as she laughed a little.

"You aren't crazy, and I am sure Elaine and Shelby both have told you that. At least now things are starting to make more sense to you as to why you left the department when you did and your life after that. Don't think so hard about this guy's name, and maybe it will come to you. You know Mack's name and can describe him because you had a longer term relationship with him. This other guy was a one-time encounter and it was a traumatic one at that. It only makes sense that you do not remember his name," Kate reassured.

"This is a very good point you make. It doesn't mean it bothers me any less though. The thing is Kate, I talked to him on the phone a few years ago."

"What do you mean?" Kate asked.

"When I was home one year after Christmas, I was at a hockey game with a friend from college on New Year's Eve and after the game we went to her mom and dad's house to ring in the New Year. I had already been drinking at the game, and I had a couple more at her parent's house while we were playing games. I went and sat in the recliner at one point and she got a phone call. I remember saying 'I don't know, let me ask her,' and then she turned to me and asked 'Hey, do you remember _____?' and said his name. I cannot for the life of me remember the name she said and it is killing me. I remember having a conversation with her about HOW I knew him, but didn't remember anything about that incident. I even talked to him for a few minutes," Kris started crying again.

"Oh, sweetie. It's going to be okay. You are going to remember, you just have to stop thinking so hard about it. I bet it comes to you when you least expect it." Kate again reassured her. "Until then… have another glass of wine," she laughed as she poured.

They stayed up until 3 a.m. and talked about nothing and everything. Kris made the quick drive back to her parent's house once all the wine was out of her system. She and Kate planned on doing dinner later that evening and sitting at the deck again doing the same thing they just finished doing, which was absolutely nothing. It was quite relaxing, and Kris could feel the stress melting away. That day, after she woke up, she and her mom met with her friend Gina for lunch in Old Town St. Charles. Kris had talked to Tony both after the interview and again before lunch. "I am so sorry I cannot be there with you right now. Are you doing okay, and have you talked to Elaine?"

"Yes to both, and don't worry about being here. I have lots of support, and I know you would be here if you could." She had filled him in on the conversation with Elaine, which in all reality, felt she had gotten more out of talking with Kate that evening than she had on the phone with Elaine. Phone sessions were sometimes very difficult and neither really liked doing them, but Elaine wanted her to check in after the interview. "So what is on your agenda the rest of the week babe?" Tony asked.

"Tomorrow I have a Reiki session to let go of all of this crap. Tonight I am going to dinner with Kate and then back to her house again. I feel very relaxed out there and feel like I can let go a lot more than when I am at mom and dad's right now."

"Is everything okay with them?" he asked. "Oh yeah, until Dad starts his crap about how he needs to kill a couple of people and won't stop."

"Kris, you know why that is, and we discussed it before you left."

"I know Tony, but right now that kind of shit isn't helpful. I would like nothing more than to see those two removed from the face of the planet, but it isn't for me to decide when or how that happens. They hurt me, and I would like to see them hurt just as much, but again, it isn't for me to dish out because it would make me no better than them. I have to trust that the system is going to work and they will get what they deserve for doing what they did to me."

"I know babe, and you are doing so well with this. You are so strong and I don't think I tell you enough. You are so amazing with all of this and of course with other things in life, but this is pretty big. Did you think of the other guy's name yet? Not to put pressure on you."

"No, I haven't, and it is making me nuts!!" she laughed.

"It will eventually come to you," he replied.

"That is what Kate keeps telling me and to just not think so hard about it. Of course that is what Elaine and Shelby have both told me too. I guess if enough people are telling me, there is probably some validity to it."

"Probably," he said. "Well, babe, let me call you a little later today on my way home if that is okay. I have some paperwork to do and need to get some stuff ready for a training trip in September. I love you so very much Kris."

"I love you too Tony, and I will talk to you this evening."

Kris told her mom that she was going to take some clothes and stuff over to Kate's house just in case she was there just as late as she had been the previous night. They went to lunch and did some walking and browsing around Main Street in St. Charles through antique shops and little unique stores. After that they went to the casino down the road for a while and left before traffic heading west started getting too heavy. The one thing that Kris noticed is how much heavier traffic was getting each time she visited, especially the little town she was raised in. Before there was literally one stop light in the center of town that at one time was a 4-way stop sign intersection.

Kris and her friends used to joke as teenagers about how the streets of Wentzville would roll up at 8 p.m. each night and 10 p.m. on Friday and Saturday. Not anymore. Now it seemed like there was an abundance of traffic through town, new ways of getting through and around the town. Kris could actually remember how excited everyone was when the McDonald's was built in town. Prior to that, they had to drive to O'Fallon or St. Charles for it. As Kris drove home, things suddenly seemed so different to her now. She drove through town to avoid some of the interstate traffic and while many of the small businesses were still in the same location they had been in for the last 40 years or more, she realized she had a different perspective. Her eyes were really open now. She smiled a little as she drove, seeing it all in a different light. Everything else felt so much lighter, and she now had more of an awareness of her surroundings without having to feel hyper-vigilant.

CHAPTER SEVEN

Kris had a really good day with her mom and when they got home, she cooked dinner for her parents even though she was not going to be there to eat it. "You know you don't have to cook for us," her mom said.

"I know, but I really do love to cook and it really relaxes me. Besides, it gives you a break and I know you will eat something other than frozen meals or ready-made meals from the grocery store. This way at least I can control your salt intake," she said as she laughed. "Now get out of my way so I can cook dinner."

"Aggravating when someone is under foot in the kitchen isn't it. Now you know why I always kicked you girls out."

"I don't mind if you are in here talking to me, just sit on the other side of the table so I can get to the fridge and stove."

Kris' dad walked into the kitchen after coming up from the basement and said, "Wow!! What smells so good?"

"Our daughter is cooking dinner for us tonight," her mom said.

"Well it smells fantastic. What are we having?" he asked.

"Pork and asparagus puttanesca," Kris told him. "And you will eat what is put in front of you or go to bed with no dinner," she laughed and winked at her mom. She finished the dinner and served her parents, hoping they liked it, especially her mom. She was sometimes picky about flavors in foods, mainly because it gave her heartburn at times, but it was her mom who seemed to inhale the meal. "Jesus Mom, did you even taste it?" Kris was laughing.

"I don't think so. I guess I need to get more."

"Try actually tasting it this time; the flavors are fantastic."

As her mom sat down with a second plate, which was highly unusual with any meal, she looked at Kris and said, "So when are you moving back home and becoming our personal chef?"

"You can always come to Virginia, and I will cook for you there, although we don't have Soulard Farmer's Market, so that part kind of sucks," Kris said.

"You have farmer's markets though in the spring and summer right?"

"Yes and they run through the fall and have special markets in November and December too, but nothing beats Soulard. Hell, very little beats anything in this area. Despite having made improvements, our zoo is still okay, not nearly on par with the St. Louis Zoo and there is very little free stuff to do. Why haven't I moved back?" They all laughed and Kris couldn't help but think of how long it has been since she has not felt on edge about something when she had been home.

"Hey Mom, I am going to head over to Kate's now if you don't mind," Kris said.

"Not at all baby girl. Have a good time and if you come home instead of spending the night just give me a call so we know to expect you through the door," her mom replied. She kissed her mom and dad before she left the house and cranked up her music when she got in the car. It was surprisingly a cool evening so she rolled the windows down as she drove the back roads to Kate's house. She loved seeing that some of the fields and land had not been taken over by more neighborhoods or at least huge neighborhoods. Her dad called them "house farms" and they had grown up quite a bit since she grew up and moved away. People still owned farms, whether they were livestock, horses, or crops, and it was still beautiful to look at when she drove this way. She arrived at Kate's house in about 15 minutes and was greeted by the barrage of dogs, two of them almost knocking her over. She loved them all but had her favorites, one of which was a Great Dane named Moose. He fit his name well but was a gentle giant.

Kate was at the stove prepping some of the food. "I brought some post meal snacks and wine. What's for dinner?" she asked.

"Chad is grilling some steaks, and I am going to do these cheese stuffed peppers for him to throw on the grill too."

"Sounds fantastic, what can I do to help?" After Kate gave her directions as to what she needed, the two stood in the kitchen prepping food, chatting, and giggling like they were back in high school. Once again Kris felt so relaxed and felt like all was right in the world. It was nice enough that evening that they set the table to eat outside on the deck, looking out over the pastures, and the horses. Dinner was fantastic and the conversation was lighthearted. After a while, Chad excused himself and said he was going down to work in the barn before it got too dark. "Don't take too long," Kate said, "Kris made dessert, and it looks delicious." He kissed the top of Kate's head and said he wouldn't be long.

Mack sat in a quiet bar, a hole in the wall waiting for Shaen. Mack called him shortly after receiving a phone call from the sergeant in charge of the Sex Crimes Unit. Unfortunately for Mack, he didn't actually get a phone call. He was not home and a message was left on his home voicemail. There were plenty of questions from his wife, because it was his daughter who had been checking messages, and now she was questioning what was going on too. The phone call alone had spurred on arguments, and his wife and children left the house for the time being. Mack knew there was a possibility they would not be back after this, despite his attempts to reassure her the person accusing him was just being a bitch, and he had no clue what she was talking about. He had to admit to the affair with Kris many years ago, and that was bad enough. His wife asked him two questions he just did not have the answers to, the first being why the hell would someone wait 16 years to report a rape that never happened? The second was, what else had he lied about if he managed to keep the affair secret for so long? He tried to explain it all away, but it had done him no good. Now it was a matter of damage control, and he needed to get to Shaen to see what he knew of a possible case. Mack had already called an attorney, and they were set to go to the department later in the week.

Kate and Kris cleared the dishes and pulled out a bottle of wine, taking it back out to the deck. Kate grabbed her laptop and turned it on. "I was thinking about something last night, and I am wondering if we would be able to look up academy class pictures. I thought maybe if we could find them from 1996, you may be able to pick out that other officer's face. What do you think?" Kate asked.

"It can't hurt Kate. Maybe it will jog my memory as to what his name is." They did some searching and came up empty.

"What is the other guy's name?"

"Mack Parkins. I know he works for the humane society now or some such shit. He used to run a training school for K-9's for St. Louis PD," Kris told her. Kate did a search for Mack and came up with a couple of images and some interviews associated with the humane society. One of them was a radio interview so she had Kris listen to it with her eyes closed. The very second she heard his voice, the tears started to flow yet again. Kate stood up and hugged Kris while she sobbed. "I'm sorry sweetie, let me turn this off," Kate said.

"No. I need to hear it Kate."

She started to wipe away the tears and as she did, Kate's son Ty came out to the deck and said hello to his mom and hugged Kris saying, "I'm sorry she made you cry Miss Kris. She makes me cry all the time." They all laughed and when Mack's name was mentioned, Ty told his mom and Kris that he had a buddy whose dad was a St. Louis Police Officer by that name. Kate and Kris just looked at each other and eventually figured out that the math of their ages would not have been right for them to be the same people.

Shaen walked into the bar and found Mack. He was not quite sure why Mack needed to see him all of a sudden, but Mack had insisted. Mack nodded at him and Shaen went and sat in the booth. "Do you want a beer?" Mack asked.

"No, I am good thanks. What is going on that you needed to meet me?"

"Did you get a call from a sergeant in the Sex Crimes Unit?"

"From the City? No, nor any other Sex Crimes Unit in the area, why?"

"I did, and I had to hire an attorney. That bitch wrote a letter and sent it to three different sections of the department, who passed it down to Sex Crimes. She gave them details about what we did that day."

"What the hell are you talking about Mack?"

Mack slammed his fist on the table, "Goddamn you Shaen, don't you even sit there pretending you don't know what I am talking about. You were there and did just as much as I did. I guess I didn't give her enough drugs in that drink."

It suddenly occurred to Shaen what Mack was referring to. He had managed to forget about it after all of these years. Now Mack was stirring, well, Kris actually stirred it all up. Shaen's heart started racing and he started sweating, Mack seeing the realization on his face. "Yeah, THAT day. Now you remember, don't you? She could ruin both of us. My wife already left with the kids because of the fucking phone call where they asked me to come in and talk to them."

"Mack, I don't know what to tell you. I did not get a call, which means she probably doesn't even remember me. I talked to her once quite a few years ago when she was hanging out with a mutual friend of ours, but she never led on that she knew anything at that point."

"Really? You are going to sit there and tell me I am on my own? You participated in that too you little weasel."

"First of all, don't raise your voice so other people can hear Mack. Secondly, did you ever really give me a fucking choice? You planned it out, you got the drugs and you told me that if I didn't go along with it, you would make sure my time on the department was miserable. What the fuck else was I supposed to do when the son of a captain was telling me they could alter the course of my time with that place?"

"Your dick got hard too, Shaen, and you stuck it to that little whore just as much as I did."

"I didn't do half of the things you did to her. Now it is time to keep your mouth shut, Mack. I only participated in the one instance. Don't you sit there and tell me that she is the only person you did this to. I have a good life and a good career, don't fuck that up for me."

"If anyone fucks our careers and lives, Shaen, it is going to be Kris. That bitch came back to haunt us, and you need to come forward before she remembers and it gets even uglier. My life is fucked up now as a result of this, and I won't be alone in that."

Shaen saw his entire life up to this point flash in front of his eyes. Yes he remembered that day and everything that they did to Kris after leaving the bar. He purposely avoided her in the station after, and the night he talked to her on the phone, he just prayed that nothing was going to be brought up. Mack on the other hand continued a sexual relationship with Kris after the fact and essentially stalked her to make sure she never said anything then. Shaen sat there looking at Mack, whose face was beat red, and he was visibly shaking and sweating. "You know Mack, your attorney is going to tell you to keep your mouth shut, and I am telling you to do the same thing. Don't call me again. I am not going to come forward and tell on myself for something that I didn't want to be a part of in the first place. I am going to wait and see how this plays out, because I promise you, if I get a call, I WILL let them know I was coerced."

"You little pussy, you always were a follower and thought your shit didn't stink. You were cocky from the get go and there was a reason people made fun of you. You and your stupid little gloves and shades thinking you were Johnny fucking law. All I did was help you find your way and let people think you were more of a man than what you were. You are a rapist, same as me Shaen, so let that sink in for a while. I didn't have to let you know this was happening, but I did."

"You did me enough favors Mack. I don't need any more from you."

"You better get a lawyer now Shaen," Mack said, still boiling not just over the situation but at Shaen for once again retreating from trouble or what could be trouble.

Shaen looked at Mack, leaned in and said to him, "Last time Mack, don't you dare mention my name or you will see what a pussy

I really am. I put that life behind me, and I don't need you or anyone else dredging it up for me."

"You better hope and pray this doesn't go any further Shaen. I will narc to save my own ass."

"You were always good at that Mack. I have no doubt that you will save your own skin while pushing someone else in front of that bus that is getting ready to roll over you. So much for the code right Mack. You know, that one that says we police officers don't turn on each other?"

Shaen got up and left the bar. He got in his car and started to drive home. He had not made it three blocks when he had to pull over because he was throwing up. He could not get that day out of his head now and knew that Mack was not going to go down alone. Shaen had to think of something. He had to keep Mack quiet.

Kris and Kate sat on the deck, listening to the chirping of crickets and spring peepers (a tiny little frog that makes a LOT of noise). These are the sounds that Kris missed so much about home. She missed looking up in the sky on a clear night, seeing the stars with no disruption of light pollution. She enjoyed the familiar smells of freshly cut grass and fields. Home. She missed it. Kris closed her eyes and took in a deep breath. Suddenly she opened her eyes and looked at Kate and said, "Shaen!"

"What? What about your nephew?" Kate asked.

"No, Kate...the other guy. His name is Shaen. I just remembered because I remember having a conversation with him about my nephew having the same name."

"Are you sure?" Kate asked. "As sure as I am sitting here, his first name is Shaen," Kris said confidently.

"Well you sound very sure. Why don't you call the detective and leave a message for him. Do you remember the last name?"

"Of course not. It couldn't possibly be that easy for me Kate. I am pretty sure it started with an "F" though and it is definitely an Irish last name." She said as they both laughed. Kris called and left a message for the detective and let him know she remembered the first name but not the last.

As they were sitting at the laptop trying to look up information about graduating classes from the Academy, Kris' phone chirped with a private number. She knew it was the police department. "Hello," she answered.

"Mrs. Parker, this is Detective Pollack. I was calling to let you know I got your message. I wanted to see if you would be available to come in for a line-up on Friday? It would be a photo line-up, and we can have Sydney come too if you want."

"That would work for me Detective. What time should I be there?"

"You let me know what time works for you, and I will have everything ready," he answered.

"Why don't we make it 10:00 a.m., if you are working at that time?"

"That sounds good. I will see you on Friday morning at 10:00 a.m."

"Do you want me to go down there with you on Friday?" Kate asked.

"I should be okay and besides you have payroll to do before you head out of town. If anything I will take Mom down there so we can go take pictures and have lunch. Would you want to meet us for lunch?"

"I can do that. How long do you think it will take for the line-up?"

"I don't see it taking too long, but do you want to plan on noon just so we can be on the safe side?" Kris asked. "That sounds wonderful. I guess you want to do sushi?"

"Heck yes. You have me hooked on that place now."

Kris sat back and relaxed, enjoying the company with Kate, Chad, and Ty. They emptied two more bottles of wine and ate all of the snacks they had. At one point Chad went up to the little grocery store just down from the house and picked up a couple more bottles of wine and food for them. It was around 3:00 a.m. when they finally called it quits and went to bed. They had completely lost track of time sitting and talking, laughing and crying. This is where Kris felt the most comfortable, and it had become a safe place for her. Although she loved her friends like they were her sisters, Kris was never afraid to tell Kate anything. She knew she would not be judged and they could talk about absolutely anything.

They didn't wake up until almost noon, and the only reason Kris woke up was because her mom called her to make sure she was okay. "How are you baby girl?"

"I am fine Momma. A wee bit hung over but doing well," she told her mom. "I am going to go get in the shower, and I will be back at the house in a while. I have to go down to the city again on Friday to do a photo line-up. Would you go with me?"

"Of course I will. Do you want Daddy to come with us too?"

"He can if he wants, but I can tell you that they will not let either of you in the room while I do it. Also, we are meeting Kate for lunch at noon. I just wanted to let you know so he can decide if he wants to come or not. I figured we can go take some pictures before we meet Kate for lunch if you want."

"That sounds like a good day. I will let your father know, and he can figure out if he wants to go. I love you very much my baby girl. Take your time over there, and come back here when you are ready. No need to rush."

"I love you too Mom. Thanks for everything."

The rest of that day and the following day were pretty uneventful. Kate came over for dinner on Thursday evening. Kris grilled asparagus and rosemary lamb chops with a red wine sauce. Her mom fixed cous cous to go along with the meal. Not much was said during the meal and when they finished, Kris asked them all if they liked it. "Why do you think it was so quiet during the meal?" her dad asked.

"I was too busy eating to say anything Kris. This was so delicious, and I wish Chad would have been able to be here," Kate said.

"I am surprised there are leftovers. We all pretty much inhaled that meal. Kate, do you want to take what's left to Chad?" her mom asked.

"Sure. If they make it to him," she laughingly replied.

The next morning, Kris and her mom moved about the house getting ready without much conversation. Her dad decided to stay home and get some things done around the house. Kris and her mom knew that it was probably best that he did not go down to the police department. He was still fuming and mumbling about wanting to kill the two involved in the whole thing, and with the possibility of running into one or both of them there, it was definitely not a good idea. They drove with minimal conversation as well and what was talked about had nothing to do with why they were taking a trip down to the city. As they arrived to the parking lot across from the headquarters building, Kris could feel her chest tightening, her heart racing, and her pulse quickening. Her unsettled stomach made her feel queasy, as she had to contain herself from throwing up right then and there in the entranceway. She stopped at the bottom of the stairs, grabbed the handle, and closed her eyes. Kris took a deep breath and exhaled slowly counting to 10, before she climbed the cold stairs that added a heaviness to her mind and body.

When they reached the next floor, Kris and her mom signed in, and Detective Pollack met them at the front desk. More silence as they rode the elevator to the fourth floor. He led them back to the unit and that dreaded conference room. Her mom sat outside the conference room while Kris followed him into the room where she had been just days before. "Sydney called and said she was not going to be able to make it today. Are you still okay with doing this or would you rather wait for her to be here?" Detective Pollack asked.

"Today is fine," she answered.

"Okay. So I am going to show you six photographs, and I will show them to you one at a time. If you recognize anyone as being the second assailant, let me know. If you do identify anyone, I will set that picture aside and let you keep looking. After you have looked at them all, I can place them on the table together, and you can make any comparisons that way. If you need to see a photo more than once, just let me know and we can go from there. Remember you are under no obligation to choose anyone, and the person you described may or may not be in the lineup. Let me know when you are ready to start."

Kris took a deep breath, and in her mind she went to the safest place she could for the moment before nodding yes to the detective. He slid the first picture over to her and immediately she said, "He did not have a mustache so any others like that you can take out. I do remember that he did not have any facial hair."

"Okay. I will still show you the rest of them," he responded. As he slid the others to her one at a time, she realized that she didn't recognize any of the pictures as being the second officer who raped her. She did recognize one or two of the officers from working with them but not as the second person involved. She could feel her heart sinking in disappointment and panic began to set in.

"I recognize a couple of the faces," she told Detective Pollack, "but not as the second person who raped me. Two of them have facial hair, and I know for a fact he did not and he was not Hispanic. He had light brown/dirty blonde hair. It is hard to see their eyes in these photos because they are all wearing their uniform caps, and he surely wasn't wearing a cap that day."

Detective Pollack had her fill out paperwork stating that she did not identify anyone from the lineup. "We are still trying to get in touch with Mack to see if he will come in and make a statement. He has not returned any of our phone calls yet. If you think of anything else or come up with a last name of the second person just call me. When we present this to the Circuit Attorney's Office, we may need you to come down and talk to them. They like to hear from the victims before making decisions on how to proceed with a case like this. Will you still be in town?"

"I can be, so that is not a problem," Kris told him.

"Well if there is nothing else, then I can walk you back downstairs."

When the elevator was going down to the first floor, Kris had no clue that in another elevator Mack, his attorney, and the sergeant were headed up to an interview room in the Sex Crimes Unit.

As they left, Kris fought the urge to cry yet again. She was so angry with herself and with them. The anger towards herself was the inability to recognize anyone from the lineup, even though he said the officer may or may not be included, and the anger towards them just compounded because of what they did to her. She knew when she started this process that she was going to have to continue to tell this story over and over again, but it was no easier than what it had been the first time she told it. Kris and her mom met Katie for lunch at a sushi place on Washington Avenue in downtown St. Louis. During lunch Katie and Kris made plans for dinner and drinks that night with Dina, Kathy and her sisters. "Was the asshole in the lineup?" Katie asked.

"If he was I didn't recognize him," Kris replied. When she looked up at Katie, Katie could see that she had more to say but didn't push the issue in front of Kris' mom.

CHAPTER EIGHT

Detective Pollack and the sergeant sat on one side of the table and informed Mack of his Miranda Rights and once again informed him of the charges he was accused of. What the sergeant did not elude to, was the fact that he knew Mack could not be arrested on criminal charges because the statute of limitations had run out. After reading him Miranda warnings, the sergeant asked Mack if he would like to give his side of the events. "My client is not going to say a word. I have advised him not to talk to you. We want to know who is making these allegations."

"And I told you on the phone when you asked that I was not going to give that information out unless you brought your client in for questioning. We want to get his side of the story." Detective Pollack said to the attorney. "Well, he isn't going to say a word."

The sergeant looked at Mack and said, "Will you at least tell us the name of the other person involved? We know you were with someone else when this happened."

"I told you, my client isn't going to say a word."

"So you brought your client down here, charging him at least $500.00 an hour to not say a word? Mack if I were you, I would be a little pissed about getting hijacked like that only to be told you can't give your side of the story. For all we know, your accuser could be lying and your story could help us figure that out," the sergeant said.

The attorney looked at the sergeant and Detective Pollack and said, "Neither of you need to worry about how much I make, nor am I only going to say this one more time. He is not saying a word until we know who is making these allegations."

"Well then, I believe you've wasted your time coming down here because I am not going to give you that information. We will take it on faith that she is telling the truth, keep investigating, and be in touch with you. Detective Pollack, will you escort them out please?"

The following week, Kris continued to stress about not being able to remember the last name of the other perpetrator and started to question if she was right about the first name as well. She had a few moments of tears, but overall she was doing fairly well. She had another phone appointment with Elaine and stayed at Katie's house quite a bit as well. One morning her parents asked if she wanted to go to the casino in St. Charles and have lunch and just play around for a while on the slots. When they were pulling into the parking garage, her phone rang and the screen displayed "private number." She answered, knowing it was the police department. "Mrs. Parker, this is Detective Pollack."

"Yes," she answered.

"I am afraid I have some bad news. I have been working with the Circuit Attorney for the last few days and we have been trying to find a loophole in the laws, but there is no way we can even file criminal charges. From 1994 through 1997 there was a three year statute of limitations on prosecuting rape. Since this happened in 1996, we cannot file criminal charges against Mack or the other officer when we figure out who he is. I am so sorry Mrs. Parker. Are you still there?"

"Yes, I am here. I thank you for the time and effort you put into this."

"I want you to know that we are still trying to get Mack in here to make a statement just to have on record. Maybe we can find that second name so you can get some closure on that end."

"Again, thank you very much and just let me know if there is anything else you need from me or if somehow you manage to get the second name," Kris replied in a business like tone.

"I will be in touch soon Mrs. Parker." Detective Pollack said, hanging up.

When Kris disconnected her end of the call, she laid her head on the steering wheel and sobbed. Her parents, who had been standing outside the car during the call, opened the door and it was her dad who squatted down, holding on to her, letting her cry on his shoulder as she had done so many times growing up whenever she was hurt. "Do you want to skip lunch and just go back home?" her mom asked.

"No. I will be fine. Besides I am starving and going back home will not change the outcome of this," Kris said. When they arrived at the casino from the elevator, Kris made a beeline to the restroom to wash her face and compose herself. Lunch was fantastic and as a bonus to what started out as a crappy outing, she won about $200 on the slots.

While she was playing around on the slots, she noticed a notification on her social media page that Ronnie Lowell had messaged her. "Hey Sharon, I have been wondering if this was you. Yes this is the Ronnie you went to the Academy with. We should get together next time you are in town." She messaged her back and told her she was in town but was leaving that weekend and would love to get together when she came home again. They chatted for a few minutes via messenger and Kris learned that Ronnie was still working on the department in the homicide division. Kris was surprised she had not run into Ronnie during her trips down to headquarters.

Shaen had heard about Mack's trip to the department and wondered what had happened. Ever since that meeting with Mack, Shaen had been on edge worrying about his name being brought up, his wife finding out, and the department he currently works with learning the truth. He knows that if Kris remembers him being there, his world could come crashing down on him. The guilt of what he did came back with a vengeance, but to track Kris down and apologize would do nothing more than admit his actions of that day. He was feeling so much anguish and regret and could not tell anyone, and at the same time, he couldn't even imagine what Kris was feeling. Shaen was terrified and even more so with the idea that all Mack had to do was say his name to the detectives working the case.

Shaen's phone rang and when he answered, Mack's voice responded on the other end. "I just want you to know that I still know how to keep my mouth shut, but I am not going to let this die as far as you are concerned. This isn't over yet and if my life is going to be on edge, so is yours Shaen."

"And what the hell makes you think mine isn't on edge Mack? We both have to live with what we did to her. The worst part is, you kept fucking her like nothing happened. How the hell can you have done that? Even worse, who else did you do that to? The more I think about it, do you know for sure Kris is the one who came forward? You did this before I ever entered the scene, and you did it later. This was the only time I did anything like this, so it could quite possibly be a different victim of yours."

"I know it was her that came forward because of some of the things that were said by the detective and the sergeant, without them coming right out and saying it. Who else would it be?"

"I don't know Mack, you tell me. I am not the one who found the need to drug and rape women on a regular basis. I did what I did because I wasn't given much of a choice," Shaen said.

"Like I said before Shaen, your dick got hard too and you had no problem getting it that way repeatedly. Whether you did it to one person or 100, you still raped her and it makes you a rapist just as much as it makes me one."

"What exactly would you like me to do Mack? We can't just take it back or make it go away. Maybe you should have thought about it before you started all of this. Right now I think the best thing we can hope for is that it goes nowhere. It's not like there is physical evidence, and all the department and court has to work with is something that she remembered 16 years later. Hell, her memory may not even be accurate."

"Oh no, it's accurate. They read me part of what she wrote in that letter and her account to them as she was making her report. Trust me, it was Kris, and she remembered in detail what happened. The only thing missing were some of the things that we said. That is how I know it was Kris that filed the report."

"Well then, I guess we just keep our ears open and see what is going to happen," Shaen said.

"Easy for you Shaen. My wife and kids are not living with me, I have a bill for an attorney that is going to take forever to pay off, and this is going to get all over the city and the department because I ran into a LOT of people I worked with on my way up to that unit."

"We both still have connections to the department Mack. We can figure out what is going on with this."

"True enough. I heard she moved away after she got married, and I know she physically came into town to file this report. Maybe if we found out where she is we can have a little chat with her."

Shaen exploded at this point. "Are you out of your goddamn mind? Are you trying to add more charges to this Mack? You don't know if her husband is with her, who she is around or anything and you want to go 'have a chat with her.' You have lost it!"

"You know what, you are right. Maybe since you are more sensitive you should be the one to approach her alone. Yeah. That is what we will do. I will see if I can find out if she is still in town."

"Mack, I really don't think that is a good idea, and I am not going to go talk to her."

"Yes, you will or I will call my attorney, go back to that unit, and tell them everything!" With that, Mack hung up the phone and would not answer Shaen's incoming calls.

The following Monday, Kris began her trip back to Virginia, not knowing what to feel. She was relieved to have everything out in the open but was still very angry and hurt that so much had been taken and done to her in one brief moment of time and not a damn thing could be done about it. During the drive home to Virginia, she contacted the sergeant in Sex Crimes to see if they ever came up with the second person. He informed her that they did not, not even from Mack. He let her know that Mack had finally come in with an attorney and his attorney would not let Mack say a word. "I want you to know Mrs. Parker that without saying why, people knew why he was there. He did run into former co-workers and to have a lawyer in tow while being escorted to our division was pretty much a giveaway. Not only did they know, but I am the one who left messages on his home phone, so whoever he lives with at this point is aware of the allegations as well. I am just so sorry that nothing more could be done in regards to criminal charges."

"You didn't make the laws Sergeant, so please don't apologize. I appreciate everything you have done," she assured him.

"Well I am going to continue looking into this to help you figure out the second person. I know you told Detective Pollack that his first name is Shaen, but we can't find anyone with that name that was in the Academy classes for 1996." They talked a little longer and she hung up feeling a little better.

Mack did some digging and by the time he got anywhere, he learned that Kris had left town on the Monday following his trip down to the headquarters building. He also learned that the statute of limitations on criminal charges had run out a year after the incident. He picked up the phone and called Shaen but had no intentions of telling him about the statute of limitations. He was a detective, all he has to do is look it up. Shaen answered the phone, "What? I told you I am not talking to her and making things worse."

"You don't have to, at least not right now. She has left town already." Mack replied.

"Just let it go Mack. If you haven't been arrested yet, chances are you won't be."

"This is far from over Shaen. I want to know why she is stirring this all up after so many years, and you are going to be the one to ask her."

"Screw you Mack. I am not doing it. Leave her alone, and leave me alone. Anything you want to do, you do it on your own this time. I am warning you."

Kris continued to see Elaine and Shelby and now worked on trying to remember Shaen's last name. Everyone was saying the same thing about not trying so hard, especially since that was the longest encounter she had had with him. It was traumatic enough that it only made sense that she would forget it. It didn't help her a lot though. She continued to think about it, and when she wasn't questioning her memory of the first name actually being Shaen, she was beating herself up for letting it all happen in the first place. Her struggle was private, and once again she was able to put on a strong front when other people were around.

She was once again working up at VCU as an instructional assistant, only this time it was for a professor in the Religious Studies Department. She was absolutely fantastic to work with, and Kris loved being able to do so. She was also still in contact with Ronnie, and they spent as much time as possible either talking on the phone or messaging each other. Kris was thrilled to be able to catch up with her and so excited to go home and spend time with Ronnie and her partner, Trixie.

Her sister Cat had given her the name and number of an attorney who may be able to help her in civil litigation or at least know of someone who may be able to help. She friended Penelope Clinton, the attorney Cat told her about, on the social media site and called her in order to talk to her about her thoughts on civil litigation. She told Penelope everything she thought would be helpful to the case. "Okay Kris, I am going to get a little more personal, because I can promise you that if you decide to take this to civil litigation their attorneys are going to get very nasty."

"Okay. It won't do me any good to hide anything, so ask away."

"Was this strictly a working relationship that you had with Mack or was there something more to it?" Penelope asked.

"Oh no. It was a physical relationship prior to and after the incident. After the rape, it was different though." Kris continued to explain the nature of their relationship and the things that had happened after the rape, specifically the way Mack acted around her. They talked for a long time, Penelope assuring her that anything the two of them discussed would not be shared with Cat. "I am going to be very honest with you Kris, if this was me I would not pursue anything civil. Their attorneys will be very nasty and bring up everything they can to make you look like a slut, mentally unstable, and a jilted lover. I am not saying you don't have a case, I just don't know if I could personally go through with something like that."

"Penelope, I really appreciate your honesty. I don't need someone who is going to fill me full of false hope or not prepare me for what can come."

"One thing I do know for sure is you have a year from the time you filed the report to file the civil suit if you decide to do so. If you need anything else from me, I will help you in any way I can." Penelope told her.

"Thanks so much Penelope. I very much appreciate your taking the time to talk to me."

This conversation gave Kris even more to think about. When she woke up the next morning, Kris emailed Derrick. She knew he was working for the ATF and had spoken to him in the past. It had been a long time since she had contact with him but thought she would see if he remembered anyone from the department. She explained to him that while he was hesitant to talk on the phone, she really needed to talk to him on a secure line. She also didn't want to email the content either. She knew that his phone lines were monitored as were his emails. She continued through her day, taking care of life around the house, cooking dinner and spending time with Tony. That night she had a horrible nightmare, something that had not happened in quite some time, but there was a trigger pulled somewhere. This one provided a little more detail than what she had experience before but nothing that gave her a clue to Shaen's last name (or the fact that Shaen was indeed his first name). She woke up from this horrible dream crying and had a difficult time falling back to sleep. The last time she checked her phone, it read 3:40 am. She woke again at 5 am to get ready for work. She had a long work day ahead of her and appointments with both Elaine and Shelby.

She drove to work struggling to keep her eyes opened and focused on the road ahead, fortunately making it to work in one piece. She had some time between work and her appointments, so she went to the lunch cart—her regular eating spot when she didn't go to 821. She was standing in the long line that was usually found in front of Mobile Munchies, when her phone rang. There was no name attached to the number which showed it was a call from North Carolina. She stepped out of line and hesitantly answered it, "Hello?"

"Kris, its Derrick Hinton. I got your email, and yes I am calling from a private line. What's going on babe? The email was kind of cryptic."

"Derrick, how much do you remember and who do you remember from the department?" she asked.

"Oh God Kris, I have tried so hard to forget that place. I don't have anything that even reminds me of it. What is it you need help with?"

"I guess it is more of a 'who' I need to remember. I know you worked out of Area II for a while before you left, and I am wondering if you remembered someone who worked in the 9th District for a period of time?"

"I can try. Do you have a description?"

"He would have been about 5 foot 5 inches to 5 foot 6 inches, dirty blonde, or light brown hair. He graduated from the Academy in 1996 and was assigned to the 9th. The thing I remember most about him, though Derrick, was that he wore these stupid fingerless, leather gloves. He thought he was 'Joe Cool,' and everyone gave him shit for those leather gloves, especially since he was fresh out of the Academy."

"Yeah, and they continued to give him shit. His name was Shaen and for the life of me Kris, I cannot think of his last name, but it started with an 'F.' Flannery maybe? Hell I don't know, and the only reason I can tell you his first name right away is because they made me ride with that little putz. I fucking hated him; that cocky little shit. Wait, are you still there Kris? Why are you bringing this all up?" he asked.

Kris sank to the ground and started crying the moment Shaen's name came out of Derrick's mouth. She wasn't crazy. She knew the name all along. "I am still here Derrick."

"Babe, what is this all about? Why are you crying?"

"Let me start out by telling you why I wanted you to call from a private line. Derrick…Shaen and Mack Parkins raped me. I went to the department a few weeks ago to file charges because I just remembered last year and have been dealing with this ever since."

Kris proceeded to tell Derrick exactly what happened to her that day. When she finished he was completely silent. "Now it's my turn to ask. Are you still there Derrick?"

"Those mother fuckers. Jesus, Kris. Babe, why didn't you ever tell me after it happened?"

"Derrick, I didn't remember that night when I woke up hours later to go to work. I just knew I woke up very sore and with one hell of a headache."

"I don't get it. Can I ask you something?"

"Of course," she replied.

"I am not doubting you, but I did ride with Shaen and it doesn't seem like him. He didn't have that strong of a personality to pull something like this off. Are you sure…"

She cut him off and said, "Yes. I am positive it was him but if he didn't have that strong of personality Derrick, it would make more sense that he was trying to please a senior officer. I have said to other people that I am pretty sure Mack had this planned out and probably for a long time."

"That would make complete sense, Kris. He still had a choice though. He didn't have to prove himself that way."

"I know Derrick, but while he had a choice, he really didn't. You remember what it was like after the Academy. Some of us just put our heads down and got through it. I got a bad rap, because I wouldn't play their stupid ass games."

"Yeah, well, this still wasn't warranted. Goddamn Babe, I am so sorry this happened to you. I wish I was there right now holding you. I wish you would have remembered then and come to me."

"Derrick, I couldn't have come to you honey. You were already married by then, and I wasn't going to make waves."

"Well, there is something else I am trying to forget," he said with a slight laugh. "I would have done something, you know that Kris. Hell, I am pissed now. I just don't know what to say. Now I really want to remember that last name. So what happened with the criminal charges?"

She explained to him about the statute of limitations. When he asked about kidnapping or false imprisonment charges, she said she already tried that route too. Those charges wouldn't work because the act was committed in the course of a Class 'A' Felony. The kidnapping or false imprisonment charges were automatically bumped down to a Class B Felony. The rape case had to be made first since it was a higher level felony charge. Essentially, any kidnapping or false imprisonment charges were cancelled out because the rape case could not have been made.

She then told Derrick that she was looking into filing a civil suit against the two of them. "Derrick, if I do this, they are going to bring up a lot of stuff from my past, including you. I am still on the fence about it, but I want you to know that you will be more than likely asked about our relationship. I just don't want to cause problems for you or your family."

"Kris, don't you worry about me. I have nothing to hide about the relationship you and I had and I would be more than happy to help you with whatever you need. I promise you that if I come up with that last name I will be sure to call you right away."

"Thanks so much Derrick. You have no clue how much you helped me today. I feel like some weight has been lifted off my shoulders the second you said his name."

"I am glad I could help, even just a little. My heart is just breaking for you right now Babe. If you need anything else at all, I want you to call me. Understand?" She laughed at the tone in his voice. "I can tell you are the daddy of a little girl," she said.

"Oh, Lord. Don't even get me started."

"It will only get worse Derrick. She will become a teenager," she said laughing.

"While it is good to hear you laugh, fuck you Kris," he responded with as much laughter as she projected. "It really is good to hear you laugh Kris. I have to tell you, I am honored that you were able to open up to me about this, especially since it has been so long since we have talked."

"I appreciate you indulging me in listening and being able to help me. Just as an FYI, the line is really long, and my dad is at the head of it. If you can push your way to the front, good for you." They both laughed, knowing exactly what she was talking about. "I will talk to you soon Kris. Call if you need anything."

"I will Derrick. Thanks again."

As she hung up the phone she swore she heard Derrick mumbling something about needing to take a road trip soon. The phone call was some kind of validation, and the tears of relief came quickly. Now she was much closer to knowing who she would be dealing with in the long run. By the time she was off the phone, there was a lull in the line for Mobile Munchies so she went to order her food. Jahn and Kathleen were standing outside the food cart taking a break and when she approached, Kathleen hugged her. "I am not sure what that was about, but I feel like you needed that," Kathleen said.

"Thanks. I did," she said as she filled them in on the conversation while waiting for her food and drink. Kris sat there until it was time to meet with Elaine and Shelby. They talked about everything and nothing, talked to other customers, and had some good laughs. "Okay you two, it is time for me to go get my head shrunk."

"Do you need a refill on your drink?" Kathleen asked.

"Heck yes!"

CHAPTER NINE

Her appointments went well, aside from Elaine once again announcing that she would not be continuing with her practice. "I will be here much longer than the first time though. I don't anticipate ending until the end of the year. I will have my phone number until at least June of next year as well."

"Well I can handle that news a little better than I did the first time," Kris said. She told Elaine about the conversation she had with Derrick and about not 'feeling crazy' about the name anymore.

"So you were correct about the first name all this time," Elaine reassured.

"Yes. It is very helpful, and now I just need to figure out the last name."

"I am sure it will come to you at some point or you will talk to someone who can help you. Maybe it will come to Derrick too."

"I may call my friend Ronnie. She is working in the Homicide Division, and she may be able to help me. I really have a lot to think about at this point. I know I can file a civil suit, and I am not afraid to have anyone else dive into my life. I have done some things I am not proud of, but everything is a learning experience. I have sure as hell learned a lot over the years, no doubt about that," Kris said.

"That is a pretty big decision to make, but know that if you decide to go through with a civil suit, you have a lot of people in your corner and a lot of support. I will help you in any way I can. I want you to know that if you do, yours is not the only life the other side will be diving into, and there are some red flags on my end too," Elaine told Kris.

"So I won't be the only person they are trying to discredit?"

"Of course not. One of the first things they will accuse me, Shelby, and Adrienne of is being biased and lying for you, because we have all seen you at some point in time or another for treatment, and since you paid us, naturally we will say anything, right? At least that is what THEY will say."

"I guess that makes sense," Kris said.

"Make sure you don't make this decision with the thought of taking care of everyone else Kris. You have to take care of you, and do what is best for you. We can all take care of ourselves, but understand that you are not going to be alone at any point in this process. They will be pointing at all of us saying '...and you're a whore and you're a whore...'" Elaine said laughing.

Kris was laughing too, but she knew Elaine could see her concern for everyone else. "Yeah, Derrick even told me not to worry about the possibility of them calling him and asking about our relationship. I told him I did not want to make waves with his family, but he didn't seem too concerned about it. I just wish someone would tell me what I need to do," Kris told her.

"Well you know what I am going to tell you to do."

"Yeah, yeah. Journal it. You know, this is your fault for my remembering this in the first place," Kris said with a hint of laughter.

"I know. Therapists are so evil, aren't they?"

"Well, now that you bring it up." They both laughed as Kris gathered up her stuff to leave.

"I will see you next week then," Elaine replied.

Kris' drive home was a little lighter. Her conversation with Derrick had grounded her, and she felt in a much better place than she had been. It was always good to hear his voice, and she honestly missed him a great deal sometimes. Things had been rough over the last few years with Tony, but she was trying. He was seeing a therapist on his own but based on what Tony relayed to Kris, it seemed that the therapist was excusing a lot of Tony's past behaviors and directing the "blame" toward Kris. It was times like these when Kris often wondered what could have been, had she not been so afraid to be in a relationship with Derrick. She did tell Tony about the phone conversation with Derrick. Mainly because she did not like to keep things from him, and because there was a possibility that they would be in contact had Kris made the decision to file civil litigation. She didn't want any awkwardness between them all. Tony knew about the relationship between Kris and Derrick, and he shared that at no time had he ever felt threatened by it.

In August, Kris had started seeing Adrienne and in September, Kris and Tony started seeing her for couples counseling too. Kris was also seeing Elaine but was starting to transition back to Adrienne as her main therapist. Once again Elaine had told Kris that she would be leaving her practice, only this time it was more permanent. Elaine had anticipated that she would close her practice by December that year. During this time, Kris had made the decision to see what actions could be taken civilly against Mack and the other officer (once she knew his full name). She spoke to Penelope on messenger and was given the names of a few different attorneys. Kris called and left a message for one attorney. When he called back, Kris spoke to him at length and set up an appointment to see him when she visited St. Louis again in March.

During one of her sessions with Elaine, she told her of the plans to speak to an attorney and while Elaine once again expressed support for Kris, Kris could also see a little nervousness around the possibility of being subpoenaed. "I know we talked about the possibility of your doing that. Have you made a definitive decision? Because again, you know Kris, the attorneys these two get will do everything they can to discredit you. We also talked about how they will also try to discredit me, Adrienne, and Shelby. "

"I know they are going to bring up all kinds of crap on me and make me look like the biggest slut that walked the earth, but I don't care. They have done more damage imaginable, and I have been dealing with this on an emotional basis for quite some time now. What does it matter? It isn't like anything they say about me is going to be untrue. I slept around for a while when I was single, Tony and I tried the swingers lifestyle for a while and I have been in therapy for quite some time. I know I am not crazy, that I have PTSD and anxiety related to it, but there is a large portion of it that is a result of what they did to me."

"Well I will provide you with anything you or your attorney needs to help you and will be there for you as well. You are sounding strong and confident, and I am glad to hear it. How are things going with Adrienne?"

"They are going quite well. Of course I am starting over a little bit, but since she already had my background it was a little easier to jump into the heavy stuff. She is also finishing up her EMDR training too, so I will just get everything there instead of having to come up to Richmond."

"If you want, we can drop to every other week until I close my practice," Elaine said.

"That would be fine with me," Kris told her. Kris could still sense a lot of tension from Elaine over the conversation of civil litigation.

"Elaine, I know you told me not to worry about other people when it came to my decision to file civil litigation, but I am getting a very uneasy feeling from you. You mentioned red flags during our last conversation. Are we talking the transition from yellow to red or hurricane warning flags? No offense, but I have enough to think about going into this and I think it is best to warn the attorney before anything gets started."

"It will be okay, it is nothing that will devastate your case, but it is enough that the other side will try to use it," Elaine explained.

"Okay," Kris replied with some hesitancy. They finished their session and planned another date for two weeks later. Kris did not have a good feeling when she left Elaine's office. She could not think about it though and had to worry about what lied ahead of her concerning possible litigation.

December, 2013/March, 2014

Kris had been in contact with an attorney in St. Louis and made an appointment to speak with him when she went home in March. December 1 would be her last appointment with Elaine. She and Tony had decided to go up to Richmond and have lunch after the appointment which was a Sunday. During her appointment with Elaine, she told her that she had spoken with the attorney and planned to meet with him in March. "I will have this same phone number through the summer of next year, so anything you need for the attorney just let me know. I am sure Shelby will be do the same thing," Elaine told her.

"I have to admit, Elaine, the prospect of all of this is very scary. It will mean that eventually I have to meet with at least Mack. Maybe by that point he will have come to his senses and opened his mouth about Shaen too. Remembering what I knew about Mack, there is no way he is going to stand alone in a lawsuit."

"Is being in proximity with Mack the only thing that scares you?"

"Oh God no! If I was insistent about my parents not being in the court for criminal proceedings, I am beyond adamant that they will NOT be there during a civil proceeding. I KNOW what is going to come out in there, and no chance in hell will they sit there and listen to this. I will have to go through what happened in detail again which is exhausting in itself. I don't want my parents to sit there and listen to that AND listen to one or more attorneys rip me apart and paint me in an unfavorable light. You and I have talked before about the shit I have done over my life and I have been very forthcoming about all of it, but that doesn't mean my parents have to hear it. My dad already wants to kill them, there is no reason to give him more ammunition to work with."

"Do you feel like you are hiding who you are from them? Doesn't that seem a little dishonest?"

"What the hell?!?!"

"You can't get overly emotional when questions like those are asked of you Kris. The attorney will be much worse and very invasive. You're going to have to reign in your emotions on some of their questions."

"It's one thing for an attorney to ask and accuse me of being fake, it's another for my fucking therapist to do it. For the record, sure I am hiding part of who I am, but it isn't for me or because I want the world to think I am a perfect angel. I don't even care if my parents think I am not perfect. Hell they raised me, but I will be damned if they get to hear every nitty gritty detail of my life and what I have done when it comes to sexual encounters and my relationships. Is it dishonest? No. It is self-preservation because knowing what you know about my parents, do you think I would EVER hear the end of it?"

"Okay. At least you were able to calm down and think about an answer. You need to be able to do that in a courtroom or in front of any attorneys taking a statement," Elaine said while expressing her concern.

"You know Elaine, while I was always nervous sitting up in the witness stand, I knew how to conduct myself in court and in a deposition. I have done them many times," Kris replied.

"I know you have, but they will use your emotions and anger against you every chance they get and while myself, Shelby, and Adrienne will more than likely be there for you, we cannot do anything to help you in that courtroom. That is all I am trying to point out. I am not trying to upset you." Kris thought for a minute and knew that Elaine was right.

"You are right, and I am sorry. I need to not be so reactive to the attacks or perceived attacks."

"Kris, you've got this. You are so strong and so damn brave. There are not enough words to describe how you have handled all of this."

"Right, I mean I could have become a serial killer or some shit," Kris giggled. Elaine did her best to stifle a laugh, as she put her head down and shook it. She knew that Kris was referring to a conversation they had some time ago on a completely different matter.

The final appointment ended on a high note and Elaine told her once again to call and keep her up-to-date on the potential suit and if she needed anything sent to the attorney. When she left the office, she and Tony went to lunch at a place right next door. They were going to go to Maymont Park but it had started snowing and were not really prepared for walking around in that type of weather. Instead, they went home and built a fire, and snuggled up on the couch with the puppies and kitties while they watched movies.

Mack had been busy over the previous months, looking into Kris and what she had been up to since leaving St. Louis the last time. He found out where she worked, where her husband worked, and the name of her therapists. He knew that there would be a record of her sessions and figured out which one would have the most information and had to figure out a way to keep it all from getting out. He obtained her phone numbers and her business and home address. Mack knew he would have to be careful when it came to sending anything in the mail because not only would it show where it came from, but if traced back to him, he could be facing federal charges and that is the last thing he needed at this point. He would get to her though and he would make sure she kept her damn mouth shut, hell he needed them all to keep quiet, especially if Kris decided to try and sue him in civil court. His attorney had already warned him about that possibility and they had started digging up as much shit on Kris as they could. He was not going down without a fight.

Mack blocked his number and dialed his phone. It rang a couple of times and the person on the other end answered. "This is Elaine."

"Elaine Hutchins?"

"Yes. Can I help you?"

"Yes, you can keep your fucking mouth shut in regards to Kris and the information she has been spilling to you for the last couple of years."

"Who the hell is this?" Elaine asked, but the phone disconnected before she was given an answer. Two days later he called the other number he had for Elaine. "Hello?" she answered. "Elaine, I just want you to know that if you do not make Kris' therapy notes disappear there are going to be some serious issues for you," Mack told her.

"Look, I don't know who you think you are, but I don't have any client by the name of Kris."

"Sure you do, I know for a fact you do. She was Kris Clarke when I worked with her and now she is Kris Parker. I also know she has been spouting some bullshit about how another officer and I drugged and raped her. You need to make everything she told you disappear. If you don't I will make life very miserable for you."

Elaine grew angrier, but at the same time was very nervous. She had guessed after the first phone call that the caller was Mack. Kris had told her on more than one occasion what he was like and that she was pretty sure he had planned the entire incident. It only stood to reason that he would be bold and dumb enough to call and threaten anyone to save his skin. "I am going to tell you this one more time sir, I do not have any clients by the name of Kris," she responded.

"Well you don't anymore, but you did. See, I even know that you are no longer practicing. I know where you currently work, I know where you live and I know some things about you that I will make sure come to light if that bitch even thinks about taking this another legal route. I will make sure my attorney knows, and calls you and everyone Kris knows into court, and he'll rip into you all, and tear you up. You won't be able to get a driver's license by the time I am finished with you lady."

Elaine was quiet, and now angry out of fear. How the hell could he possibly know about her past? Since he knew who she was and that Kris had been her client, Elaine let him know that she knew him as well. "Let me tell you something Mack, yes I know who you are too. You can threaten me all you want, but I no longer see Kris and I have no idea what she is doing at this point. What I will do is tell HER that you're calling me and anyone who knows what you did to her, and you're threatening us all. Then I will call the police department and file charges against you."

"No Elaine, I don't think you will, because before I start with you, I will go for your mom first. And don't think for a minute anyone will believe you at that police department. I will make sure they think you are as crazy as Kris is. Make those notes disappear. I will be in touch periodically to make sure she hasn't contacted you for them and if she has, they better not be given to her." And with that final threat, the phone went silent.

Elaine was quite sure he planned to follow through with his threats. She had to think of something because she knew exactly what Kris' intentions were and needed to protect not only Kris but herself and her mother.

The next few months went by, and Kris continued to see Adrienne. There were some weeks when Kris would see her twice a week so they could also do EMDR therapy in conjunction with "regular" therapy. At the end of February, Kris called the attorney she was meeting with in March to find out what he would like her to bring with her to the meeting. "If you can get the records from your therapists, the portion of your journal when you remembered the incident. Wait, did you date that?" he asked.

"Yes of course I did," Kris told him.

"Okay bring that with you and either I can get a copy of your police report or you can."

"I can pick it up on my way into town. I have to pass through the downtown area anyway." "Fantastic, I will see you in a couple of weeks."

Kris called Elaine and Shelby's numbers and left messages. She was seeing Adrienne later that week but emailed her so she could let her know what was needed for the attorney and pick it up from her. Elaine called Kris that evening. "Kris, this is Elaine. I got your message and wanted to let you know that I will not be able to provide you with the notes because I shredded them after our sessions ended," Elaine told her.

"I'm sorry, you did WHAT?!?!" Kris was beyond shocked.

"Well, I didn't think there was anything of pertinence in them and they would not be useful to you," Elaine responded.

"I have no clue what to say right now. I don't know how you think there was nothing useful in there. My attorney needs them if I decide to proceed with a civil case."

"Well most of the memory recovery work was done with Shelby, so she would be your best bet for any records." Kris sat in disbelief. She could not believe what she was hearing at this point.

"Okay Elaine, whatever," and hung up the phone. She called Shelby again and left another message. When Tony came home, she told him about the conversation with Elaine.

"Don't worry about it right now babe. Just let the attorney know, and he will handle it. If she has to be called to court, she will have to explain why she got rid of it. Talk to Adrienne about it too and see what she says. Maybe she can figure out what the hell is going on."

When Kris went to see Adrienne, she told her about what happened. "Are you kidding me? That really upsets me. What was she thinking? She knows we are supposed to keep records on clients for six years unless the client wants them."

"Wait. You mean to tell me, I can have my own records?" Kris asked.

"Of course you can. They are your records. Just like medical records. You can have whatever you want. I will call her and see what I can do. Theoretically I should have them to help me figure out where you are and what you were doing in your therapy with her. On that note, here is a letter to take to your attorney. I will of course give up any records that he may need, but I don't want to give them too early if that is okay with you. I would rather get the subpoena for them, that way they aren't 'out there'. Does that make sense?"

"Absolutely. Just don't shred them first," Kris and Adrienne laughed.

"Don't worry Kris, we will get to the bottom of this."

"Thanks Adrienne. At least I know someone is behind me and willing to support me."

"You have more support than you realize Kris. I promise. Have you heard back from Shelby at all?"

"No, now that you mention it."

"Okay. I will call her too. Tell me what else you have on the agenda for when you go home? Are you going to do anything fun while you are there?" They continued to talk and Kris filled her in on the plans she had made with her friends and family while she was there.

CHAPTER TEN

That following week, Kris was on her way to St. Louis yet again. She had managed to get in touch with Ronnie and make some plans to get together a few times while she was home. She had also gotten back in touch with Wanda and was looking forward to seeing her as well. The drive home was pretty peaceful and the weather was pretty good. She enjoyed taking road trips with Tony, but sometimes it was nice to just relax, turn up the radio as loud as she wanted and if the weather was nice enough, roll down the windows. She knew she was going to be making the journey again in May for her youngest nephew's graduation, only this time Tony would be with her. He had to fly out before she drove back, but at least she would not be alone the entire time.

As she drove into the city, she stopped by the headquarters building to go to the records division. She figured she would do that on her way in so she didn't have to make another trip just for that. As she climbed the stairs into the building, her stomach started doing flip flops. Just as she reached the door, two men in suits were coming out and the one said "Kris? Kris Clarke?"

Well fuck, she thought. Those assholes are having me watched and tracked. Now she was really getting nervous. "Yes," she said as she turned around.

"It's Terry Chaney."

"Holy shit!!!" she said as she hugged him. "How the hell are you?"

"Fine. You remember Benny Jackson, right?"

"Of course I do. It has been forever. What division are you guys with now?"

"Homicide. We work with Ronnie Lowell too."

"That is fantastic. I am actually going to see her while I am home visiting."

"What are you doing down here today? She is off if you don't already know."

"Yeah, I am here to pick something up from records," she told them.

"What have you been up to? Last I remember hearing you went out to Wentzville to work."

"I got married not long after that, moved to San Diego, and now we live in Virginia. I am studying Forensic Anthropology and hoping to go to grad school soon. I would eventually like to consult with the military and police departments."

"What is Forensic Anthropology?" Benny asked. She explained to them what it was and how it would apply to working with police departments.

"That is pretty cool," he said. "I know we could use something like that." They talked a little longer and then said their goodbyes.

She walked into the building and signed in, then headed back to the records division. When she approached the counter, she recognized the woman sitting behind the desk but didn't let on that she remembered her. She had worked out of the area station house Kris worked in as well. She was generally behind the front desk or in booking but Kris remembered that she had an attitude and hated when she had to work with her. "Hi. I need to get a copy of a police report. I don't have the complaint number but I can tell you the date I filed and my name." The woman must have recognized her too because she became very snotty with Kris. "We have to have the complaint number."

"No, actually you don't. I remember all too well how this is done." And she gave her the date it was filed and her name.

As the information was being typed in, she was reading the report and said to Kris. "This incident happened in 1996?"

"Yes."

"And you are just NOW reporting it?" she scoffed at Kris.

"Yes, but then again if you would read the ENTIRE report, you would see that I JUST remembered it last year. But that tends to happen when you are drugged to the point of not remembering things hours after they happen. NOT that is it any of your business. Can I please get a copy of my report?"

"I'm sorry but there is some kind of flag on here, and I cannot give it to you. I need to get in touch with my supervisor and she is already gone for lunch. Hang on and let me show this to my co-worker. I have never seen this before." From what Kris could see, there was a "flag" on the report. She couldn't read it, but she knew from experience it was not going to be a good thing. At this point both women were looking at it.

"Yeah, I have no clue. I have never seen this before either. We are going to have to get a supervisor's approval to give you a copy."

"No, as the victim of this crime and according to the Sunshine Law, I can obtain a copy of a report I filed. I have provided you with my I.D. and the pertinent information, and I would really like the report. I need it before I have a meeting with my lawyer."

"Well, I am sorry but we cannot give it to you. Our supervisor is at lunch and will not be back until after 1 pm. If you want to wait, you can."

"No, I do not want to wait. I have been on the road since 4 a.m., and want to get out of here and take a damn nap."

"Well, I am sorry. We can call you and let you know when we can release it to you, but I think legal is going to have to take a look at this too."

"Fine. I will let my lawyer know that you wouldn't give it to me, and it is tied up because this is how the department is trying to cover it up. I may have left a long time ago, but I am not stupid. I remember the shit that gets pulled around here. Nice to know that not much has changed." With that, Kris left and waited until she got to her car and out of the parking lot before her face got really hot and she started crying.

Mack's cell phone rang. "Hello."

"Hello Mack, its Cathy. She is back in town and she just tried to get a copy of the police report. It has been flagged so I couldn't give her a copy but she mentioned having her attorney get it. Since she can't pursue criminal charges, it has to be a civil litigation attorney."

"Thanks Cathy. I owe you big time."

"Anything for you Mack."

"I just need to figure out who the attorney is now."

"Well when his or her office calls to get a copy of it, I can provide you with that."

"You are the best Cathy. I will do something very special for you, I promise."

Kris got settled in at her parents' house and started filling them in on the plans she had. The first thing they did was go to a winery close by and have lunch and some wine. Her mom asked when the appointment with the attorney was and offered to go with her. "That would be great Mom. We can go to lunch and then take some pictures. I have a phone appointment with Adrienne later that day, but we should be home by then. You know I need to be some place a little more private when I am on the phone with her."

"You know I wouldn't listen in on your phone calls Kris," her mom said.

"I know you wouldn't Mom, but the reception on my cell phone isn't great and if I use the house phone, there is a chance someone will beep in."

"I understand baby girl."

Shaen's phone rang, and it instantly angered him when he saw the phone number. "What in the fuck do you want now Mack?"

"Well that isn't a very nice greeting Shaen. I wanted to let you know that the bitch is back in St. Louis, and she is going to see an attorney. This is possible civil litigation, so you better get your shit together and take care of things. I want you to get in touch with her and see if you can find anything out."

"Mack, I will do no such thing. I haven't been called in to talk to anyone, and I haven't heard any grumblings about this at all, so why in the hell would I stir a hornet's nest that doesn't need to be stirred up on my end?"

"You just don't get it do you Shaen? If you do not do what I am asking you, I will make SURE she knows you were the other person there, if she hasn't figured it out already."

"Fine Mack. I will get in touch with her, and I will talk to her. I will call you after I have contacted her, and we can talk. I don't want to do anything over the phone any more though. All of these calls back and forth are making me nervous and could potentially cause some extra problems we don't need. I don't want to meet in public either, so let me figure something out."

"Well finally you are talking like someone who has a pair Shaen," Mack said with a snarky tone. On the other end, Shaen felt defeated, but he also knew he had no intention of contacting Kris. If she didn't know who the other person was, he sure as hell wasn't going to help her figure it out. He was however, going to make sure everything was taken care of and that it would all go away.

Later that week, Kris and her mom went down to meet with the attorney. His office was near Soulard Market on South Broadway. Jim Bowers greeted and escorted her into the conference room. As she was giving him some background information, the receptionist came into the room and explained that their conversations could be heard outside even with the door shut. They went to the back of the office where they continued their conversation.

"Okay Kris, you mentioned that you had written this memory down in a journal. Did you by any chance bring that with you?" Jim asked.

"Yes, I have everything you requested except notes and information from Elaine and the police report. Elaine suddenly decided that there was nothing helpful in her notes from my sessions and informed me that she shredded everything. The records division would not give me a copy of the police report I filed last July."

"Well, I can see we are off to a good start," he said with a slight chuckle. "Don't worry about any of that. I can get a copy of the police report. I am not sure how helpful it is going to be if your therapist…"

"Former therapist now, not that it matters," Kris stated.

"It doesn't really, but the fact that she is suddenly unwilling to help is not going to be good." He was looking through the papers and said, "I used to be a prosecuting attorney for the city so I can find out why you had an issue with getting your police report. I know that most of the officers that work for the city are good people, but from what I am reading, there are a few bad apples. I had no problems prosecuting the ones who didn't do the job on the up and up. I don't know if you have heard, but a former canine officer recently won a suit against the department for sexual harassment."

"No, actually I had no clue. I keep up with some of the news but mostly when there are alerts on my phone, or when someone tells me about something newsworthy they think I may be interested in."

"Well let me take a look at what you have here and go over your options," he said as he was going through the information Kris brought with her. "The only thing I am seeing a problem with at this point is the fact that one of your therapists is being uncooperative. If we have to subpoena her, it isn't going to be good and their attorneys will jump on that quickly. Did she say why she shredded your records?"

"She told me that she didn't think anything would be useful and that none of the memory recovery work was done with her. It is bullshit of course. She did send me to another therapist in her building, but it was for a specific type of therapy that helped me from blanking out or having panic attacks when I was talking about the rape."

"Okay, well I can look into this a little more, and get a copy of your police report for you as well."

They talked a bit more, and he told her he would be in touch with her and that if she was able to get hold of anything else to just scan and email it to his office. When Kris and her mom left the building, she didn't have the best feeling about him, but thought it was more due to the subject matter than the attorney. She had concerns that he had been a prosecuting attorney for the city and still had some connections with the department. That could play out badly for her. She and her mom met Kate at a sushi restaurant on Washington Avenue downtown. After lunch Kate went back to work and Kris and her mom planned on driving around taking pictures. "Kris, would you want to go to the big thrift store down off Vandeventer?"

"Sure Mom, we can do that. We have been talking about that for a long time."

"I just want to make sure we are back for you to do your phone call with Adrienne."

"No worries, we will be back in time. She texted me while I was in with the attorney and pushed it back an hour."

The rest of the afternoon was relaxing and got Kris' mind off of everything. She got a text from Ronnie, and they set up an evening to get together. It has been almost 20 years since they had seen each other. Graduation from the Academy was the last time Kris saw Ronnie, and she was very excited to see her again. She would also get to meet Ronnie's partner, Trixie Taylor. They were all going to go out to dinner and have a couple of drinks. Kris had filled Ronnie in a little bit on what was going on but not too much. Ronnie had offered to help her with anything she needed and also tried to get a copy of the police report but was unable to do so.

That evening Kris, Ronnie, and Ronnie's partner Trixie met for dinner. They went to a local bar and grille and enjoyed a martini or two in addition to their food. The Ronnie of now was completely different than the one Kris experienced in the academy. They spent a couple of hours enjoying the evening and reminiscing about being on the streets as patrol officers. Kris could not remember the last time she laughed this hard and was able to let go of all the stress that had been building for quite some time.

"Ronnie, would you be willing to help me figure out the last name of the second guy? I think if I saw a picture of him I would be able to figure it out."

"Didn't you already do a six pack lineup?" Ronnie asked.

"Yes, but none of them came close to the description I gave the detectives in Sex Crimes. I am surprised they didn't sneak a photo of a female officer in there."

"That does not surprise me, but you didn't hear me say that since I am still working for them," Ronnie admitted. "Let's go down to the academy library tomorrow. I have the day off, and we can go bumming around afterwards if you want."

"Sounds like a plan to me. Thanks for everything Ronnie. This won't get you in trouble will it?" Kris asked.

"Not at all. I have it all figured out."

The following morning, Kris woke and drove to Ronnie's house to meet up. They took Ronnie's car since she was on call the next couple of days. When they made it down to the academy building, Kris' heart began pounding and Ronnie could see the look of angst on her face. Ronnie put her hand on Kris' shoulder and gave it a little squeeze. "You got this Clarke. If you can survive my bullshit from the academy, you can do this. I am by your side friend, and we will figure it out together. Fuck those guys in Sex Crimes. They don't want to do their jobs and are pretending they don't know who Mack is. That is bullshit, because they all still hang out together. Mack is in the city all the time for his job, and I know they all still knock a few back from time to time. This city isn't that damn big."

When they went up the stairs to the library, they looked at each other and started laughing. "Remember passing through these doors for the first time Ronnie?" Kris asked.

"We were all terrified and too nervous to talk to each other," she replied.

"It seems like a lifetime ago doesn't it?"

"It sure does, and I am still with this place," Ronnie responded.

The same lady that ran the library so many years ago was still running it today, and she had not changed a bit. Kris looked at her and wondered how she managed to age, but it seemed nobody else around her had. She let Ronnie do the talking, since she said she had a plausible explanation as to why they were trying to find people from the different classes. "Hello, I don't know if you remember us…"

"Of course I do, Veronica Lowell and Kristine Clarke. Ronnie, I know you are over in Homicide now, but Kris, where did you take off to?" she asked.

"I am living in Virginia now with my husband. We have been there almost 15 years. I am surprised you remember me, but it certainly is a welcome feeling," Kris replied.

"Of course I remember you. I remember that entire class very well. I am not sure why, but I do. What can I help you ladies with?"

"Well ma'am, since Kris is in town, we were trying to track a few people down to get together. We have managed to find quite a few people, but one person we can't remember his last name and anyone else we talk to cannot seem to figure it out either," Ronnie explained.

"Well I just hope I can help. Who are we looking for? Do you know which class he graduated from?"

"He graduated in 1996 actually," Ronnie told her.

"Let me grab the class rosters from those classes. There are two of them."

She came back with the class rosters and handed one each to Ronnie and Kris. Kris scanned the names and there was no Shaen on her list. She looked at Ronnie and shook her head no. Ronnie did the same and said, "He isn't on either of these rosters."

"Well you know what, I just remembered there are two more who graduated from that year. I completely forgot there were two classes that overlapped with those two. I will be right back." A moment later she came back with two more pieces of paper and handed one to each of them. Kris once again scanned her list and once again came up empty. She looked at Ronnie and Ronnie slid her sheet over to Kris. Kris scanned it and about halfway down she read the name: Shaen Finney. She looked at Ronnie and said, "Yep, that's him."

"Would you like to see a class picture?" she asked. "Their names will be on the back indicating where they are in the picture."

"That would be great!" Ronnie told her. "Let me look at it first, Kris." She said as the librarian went to retrieve the picture.

She came back with the class picture, and Ronnie flipped it over and then looked at the picture. She gave no indication as to where Shaen was in the photo. She slid the photo over to Kris and for the first time in almost 20 years, she laid eyes on Shaen. It took everything she had to keep her composure. Ronnie raised an eyebrow, and Kris shook her head in the affirmative as she pointed to Shaen's face in the class photo. Ronnie bumped Kris' arm with her elbow, indicating she would talk more openly when they left the building.

"Did you ladies find who you were looking for?" she asked.

"We sure did," Ronnie replied, "Kris, I told you his last name was Finney."

"I know. I don't know why I don't believe you. Could be all that razzing you gave me in the academy." They laughed, "At least you will be able to figure out where he went and get in touch with him for the get together."

"Oh. I know where he is. He went to a police department out in St. Louis County. He didn't go to the County itself, but one of the municipalities within the county. I think he is a detective there." She gave them the name of the department and the main phone number to reach them.

"Fantastic!" Ronnie said. "You ready Kris?"

"Yes. Let's go get some lunch. My treat."

"Thank you so much," both Kris and Ronnie remarked.

"It was my pleasure. It was good seeing you both, and Veronica don't be a stranger."

"Oh no ma'am I won't."

As they walked down the stairs, Kris' knees almost buckled under her. Ronnie grabbed her elbow to steady her, and when they made it out the door she asked, "Are you okay Kris?"

"Yeah," she replied, but she couldn't describe what she was really feeling. It was a mixture of anger, hurt, and relief. She finally had the missing and last piece of this puzzle. The tears started to flow, and she felt like an enormous weight had been lifted off her. She felt anger, because it actually took longer for them to walk across the street than it did to find out Shaen's last name. "Ronnie, why couldn't those detectives from Sex Crimes have done this? I kept asking the sergeant about getting a class picture and he kept stonewalling me, telling me he couldn't get it and that things were locked up tighter than Fort Knox. I really don't understand."

"Kris, I hate to sound crass, but do you really not know what is going on here? You were with this department long enough to know EXACTLY why that picture was never obtained for you to look at."

"I guess I just thought someone finally got some balls and started giving a shit about the people they were serving, especially their own."

Kris and Ronnie drove down to get some chocolate from a local chocolatier off of Jefferson and then went back to Ronnie's house. Ronnie got called in to work that evening, so she wanted to get back in enough time to get a little sleep. "Ronnie, thank you so very much for going down there with me. It really means a lot to me that you were able to do this. I feel a little less crazy now that I have confirmation of Shaen's last name."

"Girl, you know I've got your back. I am just sorry there is nothing else I can do to help you. What are you going to do now?"

As Kris was getting ready to answer, her phone rang, and she recognized the number as her attorney. "Hello?"

"Kris this is Jim Bowers. I wanted to let you know that I was able to get a copy of your police report and I can send it to you in the mail, but I am unable to take your case. I don't really think you have a good case, and since this is civil litigation you are wanting some kind of monetary restitution. I just don't think it is going to be possible. I will draft a letter stating everything I just said and mail it with the police report."

Ronnie was hearing everything being said from the other end, and Kris responded to Jim. "Mr. Bowers, I can come down to the city today and pick it up from your office. I would like to see the report and do not want to wait until I get back to Virginia to see it." Kris was in tears at this point. She instantly scrolled through the names of the attorneys Penelope provided her and emailed the office of one located downtown.

"Sorry about that Ronnie. I have to see an attorney. This is some bullshit." She broke down and could not stop sobbing.

"Kris, we will get this figured out. I will do whatever I can to help. If you don't mind, would you make a copy of the report and drop it off at headquarters so I can read it when I get to work? I want to see what kind of crap they wrote up."

"Yeah, I can do that."

"Are you okay to drive down there right now, or do you need to me to take some time and go back down there with you?"

"No, I've got this. Driving will help clear my head."

Ronnie hugged Kris and said, "Kris, you survived what they did to you. You will survive this too. You have so many people on your side who love and support you. Don't let that Dago temper get the best of you okay."

"It isn't just the Dago temper anyone has to worry about. The Greek in me is plotting just as much, but they sure as hell are not worth going to prison for. I will have my justice one way or another."

As Kris left, Ronnie couldn't help but feel a sense of dread and did not know what to do for her friend.

Kris left St. Louis again, knowing she would be back at the end of May. On the drive home, she had already decided to start doing research for a different attorney. She was going to look through the list of names that Penelope had given her before and see what she could come up with.

CHAPTER ELEVEN

May, 2014

Kris consulted with another law firm on her following visit to St. Louis. It was all very promising as she sat in their office listening to the process, hearing the main partner of the firm, Kip, tell her he would have no issue putting her on the witness stand. He explained to Kris that she would have to be evaluated by their psychiatrist, and by Mack and Shaen's psychiatrist as well. He explained the cost would be substantial, and it could drag out for years. During the conversation, he turned to the woman Kris had contacted and asked if there was a statute of limitations on federal rape cases, then he asked Kris if she remembers them taking her across the river to Illinois. "No. We never left the state." Apparently he was going to literally try to make a federal case to try it in criminal courts.

As they discussed everything, he asked Kris if it sounded like something she wanted to continue.

"Yes. I will figure out the cost. I realize they are going to paint me as the biggest whore this side of the Mississippi River and say that I am crazy."

"Well, I need to let you know that while this can be drug out for years, if you do get a settlement, they can counter sue you for defamation of character before it is ever paid out. You have until July of this year to give us an answer, so there is a little bit of time."

"Kip, I can tell you right now that I am not going to allow that to happen. They do not get to make me a victim ever again. They have already done their worst to me." The tears started all over again.

"I know Kris. I know it isn't fair, and that is the hardest thing I have to tell anyone. I am so sorry. That is why I was wondering if we could make a federal criminal case of it. It would carry more weight if we could get them convicted in the criminal courts first. Kris, if you could get anything out of this, without going to court and obtaining a settlement, what would you want or like to see happen?"

"I want them to apologize, in here, and in front of their wives," Kris told him with an unwavering certainty.

"If I can make that happen, they would probably want you to sign an agreement that you never spoke of it again in public. Would you be willing to sign one?"

"Absolutely NOT. They do not get to do what they did to me and pretend it never happened. Somehow, some way they have to suffer consequences for what they did. If I have to shout it out to the world, I will."

"Well, I'll tell you what. I will not close your file out until I hear from you closer to the deadline that we have to file. Is that acceptable?"

"Yes, that would be fine although I don't anticipate changing my mind. They don't get to rape me in court like that. Everything else I was prepared for. I was prepared for everything they would say, having to tell this over and over again, being called a whore and crazy. Having my entire life come into question and used against me was always in the back of my mind, but to be accused of trying to make them "look bad," well they did that all on their own that day."

"I completely understand Kris, and I am so very sorry there is nothing we can do to bring them to criminal court. We will continue to research and see if anything could be helpful."

"Thank you. I will be in touch."

Kris went back to the parking garage and sat in her car and cried once again. This time it wasn't from tears of pain but from anger. Pure rage and anger soared through her veins. She waited for a while before driving, and when she left the garage, drove down towards the river. She drove behind the flood wall and then parked, just crying and looking out on the water. It was there, while she sat and cried that she knew what she needed to do.

The following week, Kris was packing up her car to go back to Virginia when she saw a strange car pull up in the driveway. Ronnie got out of the car first, followed by Terry Chaney. "You two are a little far from the city aren't you?"

"Kris, can we go inside and talk?"

"Of course we can. Is everything okay?"

"Let's just go inside, and we can tell you what is going on"

Terry and Ronnie followed Kris into the kitchen

"Can I get either of you something to drink?"

Ronnie spoke first. "Kris, this, unfortunately isn't a social call. Terry has to do most of the talking because you and I are friends and we both wanted you to feel comfortable."

"What the hell is going on Ronnie?"

Terry beat Ronnie to the answer. "Kris, Mack Parkins is dead. He was found behind the flood wall down from Laclede's Landing."

Kris felt the blood rush from her face, and her stomach lurched. She felt exactly the way she had each time Tony had cheated on her and she found out, especially the time she came home to another woman in the house.

"So, what does this have to do with me?"

"Ronnie told me about the reasons for your visits over the last few months. The day I ran into you and you said you were there to pick up a report, I didn't realize what it was about."

"Honestly, what does it matter Terry? It's not like either of those men will pay for what they did to me. I don't understand why you are here talking to me. I don't even know if I will be filing a civil suit against them."

Ronnie put her hand on Kris' arm. "Look, we have all known each other for a very long time, and you and I have been able to build a friendship since we were back in contact. Terry and I want to help, and no, this isn't just some 'we want to help you' cop bullshit. We really do want to figure out what is going on."

"When you were home prior to this, in March, what did you do, where did you go?"

"When I came into town, I stopped off at the records division, that's when I ran into you and Benny."

"Did you get the report?"

"No, Cathy, in the records office, wouldn't give it to me. She was pretty rude. When I didn't get it, I drove out here to my parents. Later that week I went to see the attorney."

"What is his name?"

"Jim Bowers."

"Go ahead. Sorry."

"No problem. So, I went to his office with my mom and when I finished there, my mom and I met my friend, Katie, for lunch at a sushi place on Washington. From there we went home, and then I had a phone appointment with my therapist in Virginia."

"What is his or her name?"

"Adrienne Shiffer."

"How long have you been seeing her and what for?"

"Off and on, since 2009 and for anxiety and marriage related issues. I had to stop for a while with her because she worked for the military, and they limited our sessions. A while after that, I started to see Elaine Hutchins and Shelby Rowan."

"You were seeing two at the same time?"

"Not always. I didn't start seeing Shelby until after I remembered the rape. She did a specific type of therapy that helped me keep from having panic attacks every time I thought about it. Elaine was strictly talk therapy. I was seeing only her until I remembered everything."

"Could you elaborate on that?"

"I don't know what it is you want to know. Everything I remembered, was reported in my letters to the department and to Sex Crimes when I went to file charges."

"You haven't learned anything new?"

"Not until Ronnie and I went to the police academy library."

"Let's get to that in a minute. Can you finish your timeline from the previous visit?"

"Mom and I drove a little and took some pictures before we went home. We also went to the thrift store off Vandeventer. That was all we did that day. I did my phone appointment, which I drove to a local park to do, drove back to Mom and Dad's and watched television with them until I went to bed."

"Why did you go to the park for your phone appointment?"

"The reception here sucks, and I needed privacy. I went to the park where I used to play softball."

"What did you do the rest of the week?"

"The next night, I met up with Ronnie and Trixie. We had dinner and some drinks, went back to their house, and chatted for a while before I left. The next morning, I picked Ronnie up and we went down to the academy library."

"What was your purpose for that visit?"

"We went down there to see if I could figure out the last name of the other person who raped me. I was specifically trying to figure out his last name. I figured I would be able to find it in the academy class pictures."

"Were you not provided a six pack of photos when you originally talked to Sex Crimes?"

"Yes, and half of them weren't even close to my description of the second cop. Not only that, but they were all academy pictures and the guys had their hats pulled down over their eyes. The Sgt. in Sex Crimes told me he was trying to get the academy pictures but swore they were too difficult to get. Ronnie and I were shown the pictures instantly."

"Did you find what you were looking for?"

"Yes, after looking at four different class pictures."

"How did you identify him with such a small picture?"

"Ronnie and I each had a picture. I would look through the photos first, and then check the names on the back. If his first name wasn't listed, we looked at a different one. Ronnie had the picture with his class. She looked at the back of the picture, checked the name, and then handed me the photo, image side up. She said there was a person named Shaen in there and asked if I could find him without looking at the names on the back. Once she gave me the photo, I looked at the faces and recognized him instantly. I pointed to his picture and she flipped it over, showing me that I had picked the right one. All the names were listed on the back based on which row and their position in their row. His name is Shaen Finney. He is the second person who raped me. He was new to the department and had been riding with Mack for a few weeks."

Tears started streaming down Kris' face, and Ronnie was resisting the urge to comfort her friend.

Terry and Ronnie sat there in silence, waiting for Kris to catch her breath.

Terry asked, "Kris, after you and Ronnie left the library, where did you go?"

We went to a chocolate place, and then I drove her home because she had to work later that evening."

"And then where did you go?"

"I was going to go home, but I got a call from Jim Bowers. He managed to get a copy of the police report."

"Did Ronnie go with you?"

"No. I went by myself. I told you she was called in to work."

"How long were you gone?"

"About an hour."

"Okay. Now let's talk about this time. Have you been downtown at all, other than to drive through the city to here?"

"Yes. I went downtown to see another attorney to talk to them about filing a civil suit against Mack and Shaen. The first attorney didn't feel I had a case. More than likely because he had a connection to the department at one time and didn't want to lose any potential income from having cases sent to him BY the department."

"What did you do after you went to the attorney? First, how long were you there and do you mind telling us how the appointment went?"

"Well, my appointment was at 10 a.m. I was there for a couple of hours, and it was fine. They thought I had a case and explained everything they would do for me and what the process was. They told me how long I had before I could file suit and the outcomes that were possible."

"When do you have to file by?"

"July."

"Are you going to file?"

"I don't know."

"You have been going back and forth from Virginia to Missouri for months, and you don't know?"

"No, I don't know." Through the reddening in her face and the heat rising, Kris finished her answer. "Terry, those two men, and I use that term loosely, raped me for hours. They took breaks to drink, high five each other, and came up with new and even more degrading ways to violate me. When the attorneys explained everything to me and finished telling me Mack and Shaen could file a counter suit against me for defamation of character, to say I was shocked doesn't even BEGIN to describe my feelings. So, no, I DON'T know if I am going to file. I have been violated enough, but this may also be my only chance at some sort of justice in this entire shit show of an experience."

"Is this the only way you would see getting justice for what they did to you?"

"No. The true justice would be for one or both to turn up dead after being raped. THAT would be justice."

With that, Ronnie put her head down and Terry looked at Ronnie and then at Kris.

"What? What is it you aren't telling me?"

Karen spoke this time. "Kris, when Mack was found behind the flood wall today,he had sustained several injuries as well as having been sodomized. He was barely alive when he was found and died at the hospital."

"What kind of injuries? Wait, you think I did this? That is why you are here talking to me? That is some BULLSHIT!"

"Kris," Terry said, "we have to look at all possibilities. You know this."

"I did NOT do this. If I was going to do this, I wouldn't have gone to see an attorney about filing the civil suit."

"But you said you weren't going to file a suit."

"NO! I said I didn't know if I was. There is a difference."

Ronnie spoke up again, "Kris, can I see your nightstick? The one you carry when you travel?"

"Yeah. You want to follow me to the car to get it? Hell, keep it for all I care."

"I don't need to keep it. I just need it for a couple of days. We need to have it tested."

"Whatever. Come on, you can make sure I don't do anything to it."

Ronnie followed her out to the car while Terry stayed in the house. She put her hand on Kris' shoulder and said, "Look Kris, I know you didn't do this. I know nothing is going to be found on that nightstick. This is just a formality, but you know it has to be done."

Kris didn't say anything as she walked to the car, opened the trunk where she kept the night stick, but it wasn't there. She looked at Ronnie and said, "Maybe I took it into the house. I swear I put it in there the other day."

She went to the back seat and looked under the front seats. It wasn't in the back either. Kris began to panic because she knew she had it. She always had it when she was travelling because she didn't carry a firearm.

"Let's go look in the house," Ronnie suggested.

Kris led Terry and Ronnie to the room she was sleeping in. The three of them began looking in places it could have been. She normally left it in a corner by the door, but it wasn't there either. There really weren't many places it could have gone, so they all three started looking under the bed. It hadn't rolled under the bed. Kris could feel her heart pounding in her head, pulse quickening, and had an overwhelming urge to throw up.

She sat on the floor and started to cry. From the corner of her eye, she saw Terry leave the room and then heard footsteps come up the stairs. Ronnie sat on the floor with her and waited while her parents and Terry came back to the room. When they walked in, Terry said, "Kris, lets go sit back down."

Her dad bent down and helped her up. "Let's go baby girl. Mom and Dad have you."

They all went to the kitchen and sat down. "So, what now? "Kris asked, "Am I going to jail?"

"No. We are not taking you to jail," Terry said. "What we are going to do is get to the bottom of this. I am going to have to ask you some more questions about what happened to you that day with Mack and Shaen, at least what you remembered. It may help us figure out who really did this, because neither one of us think this was you. I can tell you what has brought us to you, but I want to ask you these questions first."

"Okay," Kris replied.

"You don't have to go over every single detail like you did when you went to Sex Crimes. I have actually read the report, but I need to hear from you what they did to you."

"After we got to Mack's house, when he was supposed to have taken me home, I went to the bathroom. When I came out of the bathroom, he had emptied my service weapon."

"What do you mean?"

"He took the magazine out and ejected the round from the gun."

"Go ahead."

"When I tried to get it back from him, me handcuffed me behind my back. Once I was handcuffed, that is when it all started."

"Kris, I know this is hard, but can you briefly tell me what they did?" Terry asked.

"They started taking turns raping me and when they were too tired or needed to 'recover,' Mack used a nightstick on me. Wait, is that why you are wanting mine? Did someone use a nightstick on Mack to kill him?"

Ronnie spoke this time. "We can't confirm that, which is WHY we want to find yours. There was some trauma to him, and we need to test it and make sure none of his DNA is on your stick."

"I'm not trying to be rude, but I cannot make it just reappear."

"We want to see if any of the bruising matches the brass tips on the end of the stick too," Terry explained.

"Can't someone else's be used until mine turns up? Again, not trying to be rude or tell you both how to do your job, but there are lots of different nightsticks out there. The ones from the Supply Division are different than the ones we paid to have made. Get one from Supply and one that was made for another cop. Hell, for all you know, the guy who used to make them could have been the one to kill Mack. One thing I do know is, I am NOT the only person on that department he has enraged or hurt. How about another female cop, how about another girlfriend, his wife, some woman's husband or boyfriend?"

Terry spoke up, "Kris, we are looking very deeply into Mack's life, but right now, there are a lot of things pointing to you. You have been overheard during other visits making threats or that your family has made threats against him to you and having been overheard does not look good for you. Kris, I am telling you all of this because we do not plan on taking you anywhere. You're free to go back to Virginia whenever you want. We just really want you to be aware of what is happening and ask you to keep in touch with us as we do the investigation."

"Is there anything else I need to do?"

Ronnie spoke next. "Finding the nightstick would be very helpful. Even if there is no way to match it to the injuries, the very least we can do is exclude it if there is no DNA."

"True," Kris replied, "I do appreciate your giving me a heads up."

The three said their goodbyes and Kris talked to her parents about staying an extra night or two. Of course, they didn't say "no." Her mom immediately called Kris' sisters and asked if they were free for dinner that night. Fortunately, everyone was able to come over, so her dad threw some food on the grill while her mom made some side dishes. Kris went and laid down on the bed until her sisters arrived.

During dinner, nothing was said about the visit from Terry and Ronnie, at least until Kris' phone rang. It was Ronnie, and she was calling from her personal phone.

"Hey, did you leave yet?"

"No. I'm staying a couple more days."

"Good. Can I come by the house or is it a bad time?"

"My sisters are here, but sure, you can come over. Wait, is this a business visit?"

"No. Personal."

"Okay. See you in a bit."

The family sat around the table laughing and talking about when Kris and her sisters were younger. Ronnie pulled into the driveway and tapped on the door before walking in. She walked over to Kris and gave her a hug and said, "You know this is all going to be okay. I've got you, always."

"Thanks Ronnie."

"There will be no stone unturned Clarke. I promise you that."

"I just wish I could find that damn nightstick."

"It will turn up, don't worry. Wait, did you have it with you when you went downtown that day. The day you went to the second attorney."

"I think I did actually. I had it in my trunk."

"You were there for quite a while that time. A couple of hours, right?"

"Yes."

"Long enough for someone to get into your car."

"There was no damage to my car, and I heard it unlock when I pushed the key fob."

"It would be way too late to dust for prints too. Did you park in a garage or on the street?"

"The garage that was attached to the office building."

"Were there any cameras that you noticed?"

"Not that I saw, no."

"I will go tomorrow to check it out. Did you pass anyone who you can remember? Anyone that looked like they didn't belong?"

"No. A couple of homeless people in the street and people walking to and from cars and buildings but nothing that was out of the ordinary or struck me as odd."

"I am trying to think of anything at this point," Ronnie said.

Her sister, Lilly spoke up. "Ronnie, I'm not really up to speed on what is going on, and I am sure you can't tell me much, but have there been any other complaints filed against Mack? Either by another female cop or a civilian?"

"We are going through all of that. His service record, Internal Affairs reports, calls for service he responded to with female complainants as well as females he pulled over and ticketed or should have ticketed. It's going to take some time, especially with just Terry and me working on it. One of the biggest obstacles is the fact that there are still cops up in the Homicide Division who were friends with Mack and his family. They are looking to crucify the person who killed him. Terry and I must be careful what we investigate and when we do it. Kris' attempt at filing charges has already been brought up and there are plenty who think she did this."

"You can't divulge what exactly was done to him, can you?" Cat asked.

"No, unfortunately I can't. What I will say is this…the things that he experienced, I do not see your sister being capable of doing, not even with the temper I know she has."

Kris looked at her mom and said, "See mom, I HAVE calmed down. That therapy shit really works."

They all started laughing, then sat around chatting. Kris relished this moment, not because she didn't know what was coming, but because she knew that she was surrounded by people who loved and supported her, by people who would walk through fire for her. The best part was that even more people were in her corner. Her circle was small, okay, maybe medium-sized, but they were amazing, and they were all hers.

CHAPTER TWELVE

AUGUST, 2014

Kris had started working back at the college as an instructional assistant. She was developing a close friendship with the professor she worked for and with one of the School of World Studies administrators. When she wasn't working, she was writing, a fictional story about what happened to her on the police department. She had been seeing Adrienne on a regular basis, not just for her own therapy, but she and Tony started seeing her for couples counseling too.

She told Adrienne that she decided not to file a civil suit. Kris did not want to give Shaen an opportunity to counter-sue her, which would more than likely be an additional violation, just not in a physical form. Mack, of course, was a non-issue at this point. Someone took care of him. She didn't know who, just that it wasn't her.

Kris had been racking her brain trying to remember who she had talked to in public that would have overheard conversations. Ronnie had been keeping her up-to-date as much as she could, but not much had changed. They were still digging into Mack's life as much as they were digging into who killed him. This was also discussed in depth with Adrienne. Kris was terrified despite knowing she had done nothing wrong. From the time she first tried to file criminal charges, she couldn't get past the feeling she was being set up. Adrienne was helping her process everything that had been going on, helping her understand that while she couldn't get justice through the court system, she could still "get justice" as well as finding peace.

Kris wasn't blanking out anymore and the nightmares were slowing down, at least the ones about what happened to her. Now she was having nightmares about trials that never happened. She was always on the witness stand, her entire life being dragged through the mud. Ex-boyfriends were there, telling all the details about their relationships with Kris.

Adrienne's suggestion, as always, was to write it all down, journal it, and write about it in her book. She told her to do whatever it took to silence it all, packing it away in a safe and healthy way. Kris was sitting in Adrienne's office, and they were discussing the latest nightmare.

"So, do these nightmares progress further each time or do they start and stop at the same point?" Adrienne asked.

"They start at the same point, but they go a little further each time. More and more people show up to testify on THEIR behalf. When that one stopped, I had another one where there were a bunch of men trying to rape a friend and I was trying to fight them off her. When I couldn't do that, I told them I would take her place."

"So, this is you trying to help your friends, sacrificing yourself to keep them from being hurt and experiencing any pain, especially the pain you had endured, the physical and mental pain."

"And the trial that never happened?" Kris asked.

"That could be any number of things. Do you have any regrets about your relationships or things you did in them?"

"After all of Tony's cheating, I feel horrible knowing I may have caused someone else that same kind of hurt. I wish I could go back and do some things differently, but to say I regret things I have done, no, I don't. Being the 'other' woman when I was younger is the only thing and I wish I could take it back."

"Fair enough. Do you think those nightmares about the trial are because you never got your day in court to tell your story?"

"That would make sense. I didn't just want to tell my story in court to hurt them and get justice for me, but I wanted to help anyone else this was done to. As cliché as it sounds, I wanted justice for other women. I want other women to have a platform to tell their stories too. That is what me writing this book is about. It is a way for me to tell my story and let women know that it okay to speak out. Even though there will be some fictional elements, and I must change their names, it is still essentially what happened to me. I still don't feel like I am doing enough, and that leads me to a question for you."

"What is that?" Adrienne asked.

"What would you think about helping me start a group therapy thing? We can open it up to anyone, and they can talk about anything. It doesn't have to be trauma focused or centered around the same experiences I've had. I just want to let people know its okay to be vocal and provide a safe space to talk."

Adrienne had a huge smile on her face when she said, "I think that would be a fantastic idea, and I will most certainly help you. I will go through the client lists and approach anyone I think may be interested."

"I would really like that. Thank you."

"I think it would be a good thing for you too. If anything, it will help you meet other people who may have the same interests as you."

"I'm not too worried about that. I am pretty comfortable, but then again it wouldn't hurt to meet new people."

"Exactly. I will see about getting things started in two weeks. Would that be good for you?" Adrienne asked.

"Sounds like a plan," Kris answered.

Kris and Adrienne looked at a calendar and planned for the first group session. They were meeting on a Tuesday night and would do the session after her individual session. They both agreed to bring some food and snacks.

When she got home, Tony was making dinner on the grill. She walked out onto the patio and kissed him. "That smells so good babe. Thank you for starting it. What can I do to help?"

"Go hit the time in the microwave for the potatoes. I mixed up those microwave potatoes you always do. Also, just add toppings to the salads."

"You got it, love." All three dogs followed her into the house. They were pretty sure they would be getting some treats. They loved potatoes and were dancing around her feet. "All three of you need to wait until the potatoes are done. Then you can have your special dinner.

Her phone started ringing and when she picked it up, she saw it was Ronnie. "Hey woman, what's up?"

"Where are you right now?"

"I just got home from seeing Adrienne and getting the rest of dinner ready. Why?"

"Is Tony near you, or no?"

"He is outside. What the hell is going on Ronnie?"

"Have him come in or you go to him."

Kris' heart started beating rapidly, and she felt like she was going to throw up.

"Tony, it's Ronnie and she said she wants to talk with me but wants you to hear what she is saying too."

"Hey Ronnie, what's up?"

"Hey Tony. Listen, I wanted to give you both a heads up that Kris' nightstick was found. It was found about half a mile from where Mack was found. An officer found it near the flood wall. Of course, he knew what it was and then saw your DSN stamped on it. There was a hair caught between the metal tip and wood as well as some staining that looks like it was soaked into the wood. I'm not sure what the staining is or if can even be tested, but the lab will try."

The DSN Ronnie was referring to stands for "Department Service Number" and it was the number Kris had assigned to her when she entered the academy. The numbers were never repeated, so Kris was knew without a doubt the nightstick was hers. She was the only one with that number, even after she left the department. Her heart began to sink and her stomach was churning even harder. In the back of her mind, Kris was wondering why the officer would be that close to the flood wall. The street was a pretty good distance from the wall, and he would have had to get out of his car in order to go look.

"Are you there Kris?"

"Yeah, I'm here. Does this mean I am under arrest? Should I be expecting local P.D. soon?"

"No. Not at this point. The Circuit Attorney's office wants all the testing and other details wrapped up before any warrants are issued."

"So now they are really looking at me and only me, right?"

"They are, yes. Terry and I aren't. We have come up with the names of two other women who may have been assaulted by Mack. We are digging, Kris. Don't you worry."

"It's kind of hard not to worry about going to prison for something I didn't do Ronnie."

"I know Kris. It is easier said than done, but I hope it helps knowing that Terry and I are not stopping this investigation just because that was found."

"It does Ronnie, thank you."

"I will keep you in the loop Kris, I promise."

When they hung up, Tony held her as she cried. "You know if Ronnie says she is working on this, then she really is working on this."

"I know Tony. I am just scared to death. It is going to be up to me to prove I didn't do this."

"No, it will be up to them to prove you did and we will get you an attorney. What we BOTH need to do is put our trust in Ronnie and Terry and know they will figure out who really did this. The big question is…are you still wanting to eat?"

"Yeah. I better eat while I can still eat without having to think about what I will be eating behind bars."

"You won't be behind bars."

"I may have been a cop, but I guess something I have going for me is that I will be in there for allegedly killing one. Maybe I won't be screwed with…as much."

"Stop Kris. Seriously. You are not going to jail or prison. You heard what Ronnie said. They have other women they want to talk to, and they are still digging. If he has done this to other women, there is a damn long list of people who wanted to see him dead. You only wanted him in prison."

"Yeah. I guess I'm going to call my parents and tell them what's going on."

"Let's eat first babe, and we will call them together."

They finished diner and after cleaning up, they called her parents. She filled them in on what Ronnie said and all three reassured Kris she would not be in jail. They would make sure of it.

The next day Kris called Penelope and asked her if she would be on standby. She told her everything that was going on and what she had been told by Ronnie. Penelope said she would be more than happy to represent her if it came to that, but she didn't think it would. "The only thing they have at this point is your old DSN stamped on the end of the nightstick."

"What about the hair and the dark staining?"

"It could be anybody's hair. For that matter it could be an animal hair based on where it was found. As to the stain, that really COULD be anything."

"True. Thank you so much Penelope."

"You are quite welcome Kris. Keep me posted and the next time I talk to you, we can talk about retainer and billing."

"Sounds good. I will talk to you soon."

Two weeks had come and gone. Kris had been talking to Adrienne about what Ronnie had told her as far as the evidence was concerned.

"What did the attorney say?" Adrienne asked.

"She told me I don't have anything to worry about at this point. The only thing that ties me to the nightstick is my old DSN being stamped on it. Unless they get some DNA from it, they don't really have anything."

"What are the chances they will find DNA?"

"Beats the hell out of me. I don't even know if it was used on him. I know that it was in my car, and I had no clue it was missing until Terry and Ronnie asked me about it. Apparently, it was found outside, so who knows? It all depends on what the weather has been like and if it was used, and if there was an attempt to clean anything off. So much has changed in the process of evidence collection and the way materials are tested. Who knows what they can get from wood now?"

"I'm sure it will all have a good ending, and Ronnie and Terry are doing everything they can to get this right."

"I know they are. Just the fact that I have to wait like this is killing me. I just want to know what they find. I hate the fact that people think I did this. Truth be told, he wasn't worth my time and energy to do something like this. I'm a little sorry someone else did this too. I wish he would have had to live with this on his mind forever. Next to seeing him in jail, which of course never happened, knowing he would have had to live with it is justice too."

"Do you think he ever felt any guilt about it?"

"Oh, I am sure he didn't, but maybe he thought about it as his daughter grew up and started dating, but again, I doubt it. "

"Well, it sounds like you are coming to terms with that part of the situation. I'm surprised at the amount of empathy you have to be honest."

"What good would it have done for me to have killed him? I mean, think about it Adrienne. First of all, it makes me no better than he was so long ago. I would have been taking a dad away from his kids. That is not for me to decide, and again he wasn't worth me possibly going to prison for. Then again it seems that it's all a very real possibility, and I didn't do anything. Hell, Adrienne, I don't even know the last time I saw him. It was probably right before I left the department."

"You didn't see him when you were filing charges?"

"No, although on the day I went to look at the photo lineup, I learned he had been there. From what I understand, he was headed up to Sex Crimes and I was on the elevator down."

Kris and Adrienne both checked their watches at the same time. The first of the group sessions was this evening.

"Do you want to keep chatting until everyone gets here and we can put out our snacks?" Adrienne asked.

"Sure." They both stood up and went to the fridge.

"So, what do you think would have happened had you run into him that day?"

"More than likely, I would have had a full-blown panic attack. There are times I still 'freeze' when I am triggered, so my guess is, that is exactly what would have happened."

"Well, we can continue to work on that as well if you want."

"Anything that keeps it from happening."

As they were finishing up, Kris went to the restroom and the group members started to arrive. They all took seats in the office and began to introduce themselves. Kris knew instantly she would become fast friends with one of the ladies who came. She was funny and a total smart ass, just like Kris. She and her husband had been seeing Adrienne as well. She was starting in group because she had found out her husband had been having an affair, and he announced to her that he was leaving to move in with the girlfriend. The other woman was younger, and he was leaving not only his wife, but two teenage children.

The group consisted of women, all various ages and experiences; some with traumas and some just needing a place to vent and find direction in life. Having an unbiased person to run things by was always very helpful. They sat there talking, laughing, and crying…

and snacking of course. It felt good, and Kris was looking forward to the next one.

Kris drove home with her windows down and the radio turned up. She texted Tony to let him know she was on her way home. She mentioned going out to dinner and he replied, "We can talk about it." She didn't like the way that sounded but wasn't too concerned because it could have meant they would talk about where to go, not if they should or should not go.

When she pulled into the neighborhood and approached their cul-de-sac, she could see a different car parked in front of their house. Surely, he wasn't stupid enough to have another woman there and if he was, why hadn't they left already? He knew she was on her way home and would have made them leave before she made it. As she got closer, she saw the car had Missouri plates on it. Did her parents surprise her with a visit? It wasn't until she pulled into the driveway and walked into the house that she became extremely concerned.

As she walked into the house and greeted the puppies, Tony was walking towards her as someone else was getting up from the couch.

It was Ronnie…

THE WAY HOME

May, 2014

Mack's phone chirped and he looked at the number. 'It's about time he did what he was told', Mack thought. "Did you get in touch with her?" He asked Shaen.

"Yes. I am meeting with her tomorrow. Why don't you meet me at North Wharf Street? Take Branch to get to it. I want some privacy so we can discuss what I am going to say to her. I'm not used to threatening people like you are."

"Shaen, do you ever think you will stop being such a pussy?"

"You know what Mack, you can go straight to hell. I have had enough of your threats and phone calls. Be there in an hour and a half. I have some other things to take care of before I get there. If you don't show up, I will not be meeting with her, and you will be on your own."

"I will be there. Don't worry. You clearly need more hand holding than I originally thought you did."

"Fuck you Mack." With that, Shaen hung up the phone, grabbed his keys and went to the store.

ABOUT THE AUTHOR

Sharon was born in St. Louis, Missouri and was raised in Wentzville, Missouri. In 1994 she graduated from the St. Louis Metropolitan Police Academy. She worked for the department from 1994 until 1997. In 1996, she received her bachelor's degree in Criminology/Criminal Justice from University of Missouri-St. Louis.

In 1998, she moved to San Diego and then to Hampton, Virginia, in 2000. While living in Virginia, Sharon attended Virginia Commonwealth University and received a second bachelor's degree in Anthropology, concentrating her studies in Forensic Anthropology. Most recently she received her master's degree in Forensic Science from National University.

Sharon returned to St. Louis, Missouri, where she currently lives and works as a Medicolegal Death Investigator for the St. Louis County Medical Examiner's Office. In addition to her full-time work, she is currently working on a continuation to The Ride Home. Sharon is also a contributing author in *Manifesting Your Dreams: Inspiring Words of Encouragement, Strength, & Perseverance*, which was released in 2019.

.

Made in the USA
Columbia, SC
10 February 2021